CHRISTMAS *at* CARNTON

Center Point
Large Print

Also by Tamera Alexander and available from Center Point Large Print:

A Note Yet Unsung

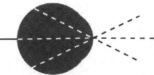

This Large Print Book carries the Seal of Approval of N.A.V.H.

CHRISTMAS *at* CARNTON

TAMERA ALEXANDER

CENTER POINT LARGE PRINT
THORNDIKE, MAINE

ISBN: 978-1-68324-577-3

Library of Congress Cataloging-in-Publication Data

Names: Alexander, Tamera, author.
Title: Christmas at Carnton / Tamera Alexander.
Description: Large print edition. | Thorndike, Maine :
    Center Point Large Print, 2017.
Identifiers: LCCN 2017035900 | ISBN 9781683245773
    (hardcover : alk. paper)
Subjects: LCSH: Large type books. | Christmas stories. |
    GSAFD: Historical fiction. | Love stories. | Christian fiction.
Classification: LCC PS3601.L3563 C48 2017 | DDC 813/.6—dc23
LC record available at https://lccn.loc.gov/2017035900

In loving memory of
my mother, June Whitehead Gattis;
my mother-in-law, Claudette Harris Alexander;
and my father-in-law, Fred J. Alexander.
We miss you every day,
but especially at Christmas.

Sarah, my love for you is deathless.
It seems to bind me with mighty cables
that nothing but Omnipotence can break;
and yet, my love of country comes over me
like a strong wind, and bears me irresistibly on
with all those chains, to the battlefield.

—Excerpted from the last letter
Major Sullivan Ballou wrote to his wife
during the Civil War (1864)

Dear Reader,

When I first visited Carnton in 2007, the history of the people who lived and worked there captured my imagination and my heart. Again and again, I would find myself thinking about these people and about what happened within the walls of the Carnton home during the final days of the Civil War and in the years following. So when the opportunity arose to write a three-book series about Carnton—the novella you're holding now being the introduction to that three-book series—I was thrilled.

Christmas at Carnton opens in November 1863, roughly a year before the Battle of Franklin. The Union (referred to as the Federal Army in the 19th century) and the Confederacy have now displaced these once united states, and the nation is entrenched in war, pitting brother against brother and tearing families—and this country—apart. Yet even in this dark time of America's history, we see beacons of enduring faith and hope in the lives of these people who shed light and wisdom on our still all-too-divided United States.

The struggles of those who've gone before us, particularly within this era of America's history, offer great encouragement to me. I'm inspired by their steadfast faith in Jesus Christ and their determination to cling to what was most important, to what truly knit them together, such as the eternal hope found in the true meaning of Christmas. I hope you will be inspired too.

I'm nearing completion of the first Carnton novel which will release in the fall of 2018. If you've not visited the Carnton Plantation in Franklin, Tennessee, I hope you'll consider doing so. We must never forget our past, first so we don't make the same mistakes we made before, but also so we might gain wisdom and perspective from those who—on both sides of the war—loved their country with a passion and depth rarely seen since.

Lastly, I wish you a very Merry Christmas and hope you enjoy the collection of recipes we've included in the back pages. I'd love to hear how they turn out for you!

Thank you for entrusting your time to me. It's a treasure I never take for granted.

Blessings from Carnton,
Tamera

CHAPTER I

NOVEMBER 13, 1863
FRANKLIN, TENNESSEE
21 MILES SOUTH OF NASHVILLE

"Very nice stitching, Mrs. Prescott."

Aletta looked up, not having heard her employer's approach. Focused on her task, she was determined to leave the factory on time that afternoon. It was a special day, after all, and Andrew would be excited. Her son needed this encouragement. They both did. "Thank you, Mr. Bodeen, for your kind words."

"You always do excellent work, Mrs. Prescott. Every stitch so straight and even, perfectly matching the one before."

She smiled her thanks despite perceiving a negative quality in his voice. Not that Mr. Bodeen ever sounded jovial. Unmarried, not much older than she was, he always seemed a sad sort. A discontented, melancholy man. But then, how could any able-bodied, healthy man maintain a sense of self-worth, much less pride, when he'd chosen to stay behind and work in

11

a factory instead of joining the rest of the men who'd left home and loved ones to fight in the war?

Like her beloved Warren had done.

Her throat tightened with emotion. Would it always hurt this much? She swallowed. Nearly one month to the day since she'd received the letter from the War Department, yet she still had trouble believing he was gone. Perhaps if she could see his body one last time, she'd be better able to accept that—

"Would you join me in my office, Mrs. Prescott?"

"In your office, sir?" Aletta paused mid-stitch and looked across the rows of seamstresses to the clock on the factory wall. A quarter past four. Almost another hour before her shift was over. Then she felt the stares.

She looked around only to see the other women quickly bowing their heads and turning curious gazes back to their work. Except for one woman. On the opposite side of the factory. Aletta recognized her. Marian, she thought her name was. They'd begun working at Chilton Textile Mills about the same time. Marian was gathering her coat and reticule—and wiping tears from her eyes.

"Mrs. Prescott." Mr. Bodeen gestured. "My office, please."

Aletta laid aside the garment she'd been

12

sewing, bothered by having to set it aside unfinished, while the greater part of her sensed that unfinished stitches should be the least of her concerns.

She followed him down the aisle, then past rows of coworkers, the click of her heeled boots marking off the seconds as the tension in the room swiftly registered.

Mr. Bodeen's office proved to be considerably more insulated from winter's chill than the factory, and she rubbed her hands together, welcoming the warmth while also trying to control her nerves. Her knuckles were stiff and swollen from long hours of stitching. But she had only to think of what Warren had endured to silence that frivolous complaint.

He'd always been careful not to reveal too many details about the war in his letters. But one night during his furlough home in April—the last time she'd seen him—after he'd banished any doubt she might have had about his continued desire for her, he'd lain beside her in the darkness and talked into the wee hours of morning. He talked all about the battles, life in the encampments, and the countless friends he'd made—and lost—during the war. "Friends as close as any brothers I might've had," he'd whispered, his strong arms tightening around her, his breath warm on her skin. "There's one fellow from right here in Franklin. Emmett Zachary.

You'd like him, Lettie. Maybe you and his wife, Kate, could meet up sometime."

She'd never heard him go on like that. So unfettered, as though the weight of his soul had grown too heavy for him to bear alone. His words had painted indelible pictures in her mind. Images she'd have wished to erase, but for Warren's fingerprint on them.

Anything from him was something she wanted to hold on to.

She'd made a point to look up Kate Zachary, and they'd even had tea on two occasions. But the hours in each day seemed to fly, as did the weeks, and she hadn't seen Kate since the afternoon she'd visited her to tell her about the letter she'd received from the War Department. *". . . slain on the battlefield, having given the ultimate sacrifice for love of home and defense of country"* is how the letter had been worded.

The notice had arrived only two days after she'd received a hastily written letter from Warren telling her he was faring well enough and that he'd penned two more letters to her that he would send shortly. The letters never arrived.

What she wouldn't give to have them now. To have him back.

"Please have a seat, Mrs. Prescott."

Aletta did as Mr. Bodeen asked, her gaze falling to a handwritten list atop his desk. Was it a list of names? She attempted a closer look

14

as she sat. It was hard to read the writing upside down, and yet—

She was fairly certain she saw Marian's name, the coworker she'd seen crying moments earlier. Aletta swallowed, panic clawing its way up her chest.

"Mrs. Prescott, you know how much we appreciate your work. How you—"

"Please don't take away my job, Mr. Bodeen. Reduce my hours if you need to, but—"

"Mrs. Prescott, I—"

"I'm behind on the mortgage, Mr. Bodeen. And keeping food in the pantry is already a challenge. Mr. Stewart at the mercantile has extended my credit as far as he can, and I don't know what I'll—"

"I wish there were something else I could do, ma'am, but—"

"I have a son, sir. Andrew. He's six years old. Today, in fact." She tried to smile and failed. "He's waiting for me even now because we're supposed to—"

"Mrs. Prescott!" His voice was sharp. "Please do not make this more difficult on me than it already is. You are an exceptional worker, and I've written you an outstanding reference. Which is more than I'm doing for the others." He pushed a piece of paper across the desk.

Numb, Aletta could only stare at it, the words on the page blurring in her vision.

"With the war, customers aren't buying clothing like they used to. And there's simply not enough work for the seamstresses we've employed. I'm sorry. You were one of the last women we hired, so it only seemed fitting."

"But you complimented me a moment ago. You said I always do excellent work."

"I know what I said, Mrs. Prescott." He averted his gaze. "I was hoping to . . . soften the blow."

She blinked and moved a hand to her midsection, feeling as though she'd been gut-punched, as Warren might've said. It had taken her weeks to find this job, and that had been almost a year ago—after she'd lost her job at the bakery. The town of Franklin was in far worse shape economically now than then. Up until a couple of months ago, the Federal Army's occupation of the town had made for a tenuous existence for Franklin residents. Especially considering the garrisons of soldiers encamped in and around Fort Granger while thousands of Confederate troops were entrenched only miles away.

But according to recent reports in the newspaper, the Federal Army had moved farther south, leaving only a small garrison behind in the fort. The absence of Federal soldiers in town seemed to substantiate those reports.

Mr. Bodeen rose, so she did likewise, her mind in a fog.

16

"Mrs. Prescott, today being Friday, you may collect this week's wages from the accounting office as you leave."

She struggled to think of other arguments to offer on her behalf, but none came. And even if they had, she didn't think he would listen. His mind was decided. She retrieved the letter of recommendation, folded it, and stuffed it into her skirt pocket.

Moments later, she exited the factory and walked to the corner, numb, not knowing what to do, where to go. So she started walking. And with each footfall, snatches of the conversation from Mr. Bodeen's office returned on a wave of disbelief. And anger. *"Please do not make this more difficult on me than it already is."*

Difficult on *him?*

She had half a mind to turn around, march right back into his office, and tell him what difficult truly looked like. Yet such a decision would undoubtedly mean she'd forfeit her letter of reference. Which she sorely needed to help distinguish herself from the flood of other women seeking employment.

Already, evergreen wreaths dotted the occasional storefront, some wreaths adorned with various shades of ribbon, others with sprigs of holly, the red berries festive with holiday color. One bold shopkeeper had even hung a bouquet of mistletoe in the entryway. But despite the hints of Christmas, Aletta couldn't bring herself to feel the least bit festive. Not this year.

Approaching the train station, she saw a man seated on the corner of the street. He was holding a tin cup. Beggars were commonplace these days, and she hated that she didn't have much to give him. As she grew closer, though, she realized he wasn't seated. He was an amputee. The man had lost both of his legs. He turned and met her gaze, and the haunting quality in his expression wouldn't let her look away.

He was blond with ruddy skin and didn't look like Warren at all. Yet all she could see was her husband. How had Warren died? On the battlefield, yes, but had he suffered? Oh, she prayed he hadn't. She prayed his death had been swift. That he'd been surging forward in one breath and then drinking in the breath of heaven in the next.

She reached into her reticule and withdrew a coin—one of precious few remaining even counting this week's wages—and dropped it in the cup, the *clink* of metal on metal severing the moment.

"God bless you, ma'am."

"And you, sir," she whispered, then continued on even as a familiar sinking feeling pressed down inside her. President Lincoln had recently issued a proclamation to set apart and observe the last Thursday of this month as a day of

18

thanksgiving and praise to the Almighty. But, God forgive her, she didn't feel very grateful right now. And it hurt to even think about celebrating Christmas without Warren.

She hiccupped a breath, the freezing temperature gradually registering as her body cooled from the exertion of walking. She slowed her steps and wrapped her arms around herself as a shiver started deep inside. She tugged her coat tighter around her abdomen, no longer able to fasten the buttons.

Seven months and one week. By her calculations, that's how far along she was.

She knew because that was how long it had been since Warren's furlough. They'd been so careful when they'd been together, or had tried to be. *Oh dear God . . .* How had she let this happen? What was she going to do? She tried not to let her thoughts go to the dark places again, as she thought of them. She was a woman of faith, after all. She believed in God's loving care.

Yet there were times, like this, when her faith seemed far too fragile for the burdens of life. She wished she could hide her thoughts from him. Wished the Lord couldn't see the doubts she courted even in the midst of struggling to believe. But he saw everything. Heard every unuttered thought. And right now, that truth wasn't the least comforting.

Guilt befriending her worry, she continued down the thoroughfare.

When she reached Baker Street, she turned right. Ten minutes later, she paused at the corner of Fifth and Vine and looked at the house two doors down. Their home. A modest residence Warren had purchased for them four years earlier with the aid of a loan from the Franklin Bank. A loan the bank was threatening to call in.

And now she'd lost her only means of support. And stood to lose all their equity in the home as well if she couldn't convince the bank to give her more time. She'd considered selling, but no one was buying. Yet when—or if—the economy finally improved and houses did start selling again, she couldn't sell if she'd been evicted. She continued past her home and toward her friend's house a short distance away.

She'd waited until late August to write Warren about the baby, wanting to be as certain as she could be—following two miscarriages in the last two years—that the pregnancy was going to be sustained. Yet he hadn't mentioned anything about their coming child in his last letter. Had he even known about the baby before his death? The Federal Army had recently blockaded certain southern ports, seizing all correspondence belonging to the Confederate Postal System. So perhaps he'd never received her letter. Or maybe that explained why his last two letters had gone—

"Mama!"

Nearing MaryNell's house, Aletta looked up to see Andrew racing toward her from down the street, his thin legs pumping. She hurried to meet him.

"What are you doing outside, honey?" She hugged him tight, his little ears like ice. "And without your coat and scarf?"

"It's okay. I'm not cold. Mc and Seth, we're playin' outside while his mother visits with the bank man."

Aletta frowned, aware of Seth watching them from the front yard. MaryNell Goodall knew how susceptible Andrew was to illness and that he needed to bundle up in this bitter weather. Born three weeks early, he'd always been on the smaller side. And despite having a healthy appetite—the boy would eat all day if she could afford to let him—he'd never caught up in size to boys his own age.

What was going to happen to him now that she'd lost her job? How would she provide for him? And, in scarcely two months, the baby?

It occurred to her then that her lack of employment would also affect MaryNell. When MaryNell lost her own job a few months earlier, she'd offered to watch Andrew—and teach him at home like she was already teaching Seth. MaryNell claimed that keeping two boys was easier than keeping one, and Aletta knew there was some truth to that statement. And since dear Mrs. Crawford, the woman who had kept Andrew up until then, had moved to North Carolina to live with one of her children, MaryNell's offer had been a perfectly timed blessing. Only four streets away from theirs, too, and with Seth and Andrew already such good friends.

Aletta insisted on paying MaryNell a small wage each week. Still, she didn't know how the woman made ends meet, having no job and being behind on her mortgage as well. Not to mention not having heard from her husband, Richard, in over three months. His silence didn't bode well. But there was still hope. And MaryNell, as soft-spoken as she was and uncommonly pretty, had never once complained.

Despite the worry settling in her chest, Aletta glimpsed the excitement in Andrew's eyes and attempted a lightness to her voice. "Let's collect your coat so we can go home and start celebrating your birthday!"

"You're still gonna make my favorite pie?"

"Of course I am." She'd saved for weeks to buy the ingredients for the chocolate cream pie— sugar, vanilla, and cocoa being so expensive and hard to come by. Now all she could think about was how much further she could've stretched that money. But it was Andrew's birthday, and she was determined to make it special. She climbed the steps to the porch and knocked on the door.

MaryNell answered a moment later, her expression revealing surprise. "Aletta! You're early. But . . . good for you. I'm always saying you work far too hard as it is." Hesitating briefly, she finally stepped to one side. "Come in. I let the boys go outside to play for a bit."

"Yes, I saw them," Aletta said softly, then spotted a man seated on the settee.

He stood as she entered and looked between her and MaryNell, and Aletta got the feeling she'd interrupted something.

"Mr. Cornwall," MaryNell finally said, her voice tight. "Allow me to introduce Mrs. Warren Prescott. Aletta, this is Mr. Cornwall. He's . . . an acquaintance. From Franklin Bank."

Tall and barrel chested, Cornwall was heavy around his middle and a good deal older. He had a commanding air about him, but not one that inspired. And although MaryNell had called him an acquaintance, Aletta found it odd that her friend couldn't seem to look the man in the eye. And since when did *acquaintances* from the bank make house calls?

"Mrs. Prescott." He glanced at her. "Pleasure to meet you, I'm sure."

Aletta nodded, but he'd already looked away. "Likewise, sir."

He turned then, and, whether by intention or not, he angled himself in MaryNell's direction, making it impossible for Aletta to see his face.

"Mrs. Goodall, I appreciate the opportunity to speak with you this afternoon, and I look forward to hearing from you soon."

MaryNell's gaze flitted to his. "Yes. I'll . . . be in touch."

He strode out the door and closed it behind him.

Aletta watched him through the window as he continued past the boys, who were playing cowboys and Indians. As her gaze followed him down the street, a sickening suspicion brewed inside her that she didn't want to imagine, much less acknowledge. But when she looked back at MaryNell and glimpsed the dread and guilt in her friend's expression, she was all but certain her suspicions were true.

CHAPTER 2

"Well"—MaryNell quickly turned away—"let mc fctch Andrew's coat for you. I know you must be eager to get home. Today being his birthday and all."

"MaryNell . . ." Aletta attempted to gain her attention, but to no avail. How did she even begin to broach such a subject? And what if her suspicions proved wrong? It could mean the end of their friendship. On the other hand . . . if Mr. Cornwall's visit *was* of a sordid nature as Aletta suspected—he hailing from the bank and MaryNell being behind on her mortgage—how could she stand by and say nothing?

MaryNell handed her Andrew's coat and scarf, avoiding her gaze. "Here you go. I hope you two have a pleasant evening."

"MaryNell . . . I realize you may think this is none of my business and you may well be right, but I—"

"Andrew tells me you're making your famous chocolate cream pie tonight. He's only mentioned it six or seven times today."

Neither the abrupt change in topic nor the

forced brightness in MaryNell's tone could mask the hint of unshed tears—and fear—in her eyes. But they did all but answer the question in Aletta's mind. And she felt sick inside.

She knew that fear, knew how swiftly life could change. So many widows, so many fatherless children. Life was so precarious. She'd asked Warren before he'd left if he was certain he could take another man's life. "Aletta, I think every man is capable of killing another man . . . given the right circumstances." Did that same thinking apply to a woman too? Could a woman commit acts she'd usually never dream of?

"Yes, I'm making that pie," she said softly. "It's his favorite." Then a thought occurred. "Why don't you and Seth come over for a slice this evening? And we'll celebrate together."

The knowing look in MaryNell's expression said she was wise to the motivation behind the invitation. "Thank you, Aletta. But . . . not tonight." She walked to the door.

Aletta followed, then paused beside her, realizing she hadn't told her the news yet. The words didn't come easily. "I . . . lost my job at the factory today. Several of us did, in fact."

"Oh, Aletta. I'm so sorry. Truly."

Aletta nodded. "Thank you."

The silence stretched and MaryNell started to open the door, but Aletta covered her friend's hand on the knob.

"If there's anything you need, MaryNell, I'm here. I'll do anything I can to help you. You're not alone, please know that."

MaryNell looked at her, the false brightness in her expression faltering only for a second. Then she looked away, taking a quick breath. "Seth will miss seeing Andrew every day. But we'll be sure to get the boys together again soon."

MaryNell opened the door and Aletta stepped outside, the bitter cold wind all but blowing straight through her.

CONFEDERATE CAMP
OUTSKIRTS OF NASHVILLE

"Hold still for me, Captain Winston."

The steel scalpel cold against his temple, Jake obliged as the doctor cut the bandages from around his eyes. "I take it you've done this before, Doc."

The army surgeon laughed beneath his breath. "Nope. You're the first."

Hearing the teasing in the older man's voice, Jake smiled to mask the tightness in his chest, trying his best not to let his thoughts go where the deliberately imposed darkness of the past seven days had threatened to take them.

"I consulted with another surgeon, Captain, who agreed with my diagnosis. Allowing your eyes to rest for the past few days, especially with that salve on them, should have advanced the healing process. Once I remove the bandages, I want you to keep your eyes closed."

With the cloths removed, the coolness of the air intensified around Jake's eyes. Even with them still shut, he sensed the brightness inside the hospital tent, which wasn't a surprise. He wasn't blind, after all. The whack on his head he'd suffered after being shot had simply blurred his vision a little.

"I'm handing you a warm compress, Captain . . ."

Jake opened his hands.

"Press it gently to your eyes. It will help dissolve whatever salve remains."

Jake complied, the warmth and moisture feeling good. He rubbed carefully, the ointment's once-pungent scent, smelling a little like bitterroot and rosemary, all but gone.

"Now, still holding the cloth up to your eyes, I want you to open them a little at a time. Let your eyes adjust to the light."

Jake squinted, then winced. Even the dimness of the tent seemed overbright. Finally, after a moment or so, he managed to open his eyes fully. He blinked as his immediate world came into view.

"How do things look, Captain Winston?"

Jake held his hand out in front of him. "So far, so good, Doc."

The physician handed him a book. "Try reading for me."

Jake opened the cover and flipped over a few pages—and felt that unwelcome tug on his thoughts returning again. He squinted. "I can read the words. But they're a mite fuzzy."

"That could be due to some lingering salve."

Jake nodded, but he didn't think so. He'd wiped the ointment clean.

"Try your rifle sight next."

The doctor crossed to the entry of the tent and pulled back the flap. The cold followed quickly on the heels of a dull November sun as Jake pulled the sight from his pocket and peered through. His pulse edged up a notch. He closed his right eye, then opened it again, trying to focus. But couldn't. He swallowed hard.

"Don't be discouraged, Captain. Similar to the wound in your shoulder, your eyesight needs time to heal. At this point, we still have every reason to believe your full sight will return."

Again Jake nodded. But the apprehension in the surgeon's expression, and the way the man looked away when he spoke, told him a different story.

A story no sharpshooter ever wanted to hear.

"I'm here to see Mr. Tanner, please." Aletta attempted to appear composed while Andrew tugged on her hand, doing his best to pull away. But she noticed other patrons in the bank beginning to stare.

The young woman behind the desk glanced down at an open ledger. "And do you have an appointment, Mrs. . . . ?"

"Prescott. And yes, I do, of a nature." Aletta shot her son a last look of warning. "I came by on Monday, three days ago, and spoke with Mr. Tanner. He told me he needed to meet with the board about my situation. Then he asked me to stop back by today for their response."

The young woman nodded, but Aletta didn't find her frown particularly comforting.

"Wait here, please, Mrs. Prescott."

The secretary disappeared into Mr. Tanner's office and closed the door behind her.

Andrew tugged harder. "This isn't any fun!"

"Not everything can be fun, Andrew. Now hold still. This won't take long."

Or at least she hoped it wouldn't. Mr. Tanner had given her strong reason to believe that the board would, under the circumstances, extend her more time to pay the mortgage. She prayed he was right.

"Mrs. Prescott . . ."

Aletta turned. "Oh, Mr. Tanner! Thank you, sir, for seeing me."

"Most certainly." He gestured. "Why don't we meet in my office? That will allow us more privacy."

She felt a twinge of uncertainty at his suggestion but worked to maintain her optimism, while also working to keep hold of Andrew. The boy couldn't seem to stay still. His unruliness reminded her of the first weeks after Warren had left to fight over two years ago. Andrew had constantly challenged her. Much as he'd done in recent days while she'd scoured the town of Franklin looking for work—with no success. He'd been obstinate and resentful. Not that she could blame him. His world had been upended yet again. He needed the loving influence and firm hand of his father.

A father who was never coming home.

She claimed one of two chairs opposite Mr. Tanner's side of the desk, and Andrew took the other while eyeing a candy dish on the bank officer's desk. In a blink, Andrew hopped down, grabbed a piece of peppermint, and popped it into his mouth before she could react.

"I'm sorry, Mr. Tanner," Aletta whispered, assisting Andrew back into his chair with a scolding glance. "Andrew, we must ask permission first." She placed a restraining hand on her son's leg before turning back. "Candy is a rarity these days, sir."

"It's not a bother, Mrs. Prescott. Tell me, have you had success with securing employment?"

"No, sir, not yet. But I won't give up," she

added quickly, her smile feeling brittle. "I'm hoping to find something soon."

"I share that same hope, ma'am." He cleared his throat. "Allow me to come directly to the point, Mrs. Prescott."

He hesitated, and her heart fell.

"The board of officers met," Mr. Tanner continued, "and . . . unfortunately, given your present situation and lack of employment, they do not believe that granting you more time to bring your loan current would be prudent. Nor practical. I'm so sorry."

The sincerity in his voice worked to undermine her already tenuous emotions.

"Therefore, the board voted to proceed with the foreclosure. But I *was* able to persuade them to allow you and your son more time before you must vacate the home."

Vacate their home. She took a deep breath, the ache of missing Warren in that moment nearly unbearable. "Thank you, Mr. Tanner. That's something, at least."

"They granted you until the first of December to find somewhere else to live."

"Two weeks?" The scant relief she'd felt evaporated, and a rush of anger that had been building in recent days erupted. "That's *all?* We have to leave the home we've lived in—and have faithfully made payments on for almost four years—in only two weeks? And my late husband

so recently—" She caught herself. "—having sacrificed everything for his country, and this is the decision you make? This is the step the board would take if it involved one of their wives? Their children? You would push them from their home and into the streets?"

Andrew cocked his little head. "We're not gonna live at home anymore, Mama?"

Confusion riddled his expression, and Aletta wished again that she hadn't had to bring him along. But leaving him with MaryNell wasn't an option at present. "Everything will be fine, sweetheart," she said softly, wishing she believed it. She turned back and sighed. "My apologies to you, Mr. Tanner. Focusing my anger toward you is out of line. I know you did all you could. It's simply . . . two weeks is not a very long time. Especially for a woman . . . in my circumstance."

Mr. Tanner briefly bowed his head. "I understand, Mrs. Prescott. And may I offer, again, my sincere condolences on your loss. I, too, am sorry. I held such hope that this would turn out differently."

She heard the finality in his voice and started to rise—when Andrew lunged again for the candy dish. She swiftly grabbed his arm. But not before he snatched a handful of peppermints. He yanked away from her, hitting the candy dish and sending it crashing to the floor. Shards of glass and peppermint scattered everywhere.

Heat poured through her. "Oh, Mr. Tanner! I'm so sorry! Allow me to help clean this up." She rose, holding on to Andrew while already calculating how to kneel, something that was becoming more of a challenge.

"Don't worry yourself over it, Mrs. Prescott. Please. My secretary will see to it."

He crossed to the door and opened it, a clear message sent in the act. Trying to regain her composure, Aletta followed, Andrew in hand. She couldn't bring herself to look up at Mr. Tanner as they exited.

"Thank you for your time, sir."

They were nearly to the front door of the bank when Andrew tugged hard and attempted to turn back. But Aletta was having none of it, her grip viselike.

"Andrew, I told you—"

"There's Mrs. Goodall's friend." Andrew pointed.

Sure enough, Aletta turned and spotted the man she'd seen at MaryNell's house last week. He was seated behind a large desk in an office near the center of the bank. Her gaze went to the shingle hanging above the door, and the truth expelled the breath from her lungs.

Herbert Cornwall, President, Franklin Bank.

The man happened to look up, and their eyes met. His gaze deepened in recognition, and Aletta felt the heat of indignation rush through her.

She still hoped her suspicions were mistaken. However thin that hope was. So much about this world was wrong, and unjust, and didn't seem at all to be moving in the right direction. What kind of world would her son—her *children*—grow up in? She didn't know. She only wished they could have had their father alongside them as they did.

She turned and strode from the bank, Andrew in tow.

"You want one?" he said after a minute. "I'll share."

She looked down to see him extending his hand, two peppermint candies nestled in his sticky palm.

"Mr. Tanner sneaked 'em to me as we left," he said quickly. "I promise."

Reading honesty in his eyes, she took one of the candies and popped it into her mouth, the cool rush of sweetness nearly overwhelming her taste buds.

"It's good. Huh, Mama?"

She nodded, seeing Warren in his expression, and cherishing both of them.

"News from the War Department!" a newspaper boy called out from the corner.

Unwilling to part with another precious coin given her circumstances, she still wanted to read that list. Some would call her foolish, she realized. But she'd heard of a woman who had received notification of her husband's death only to read his name sometime later in the War Department's updates—where he was listed as having been wounded in battle and was still very much alive.

She spotted three women huddled close around a newspaper and waited, understanding their heartache, as, gradually, relief smoothed a measure of the worry from each of their expressions. One of the women happened to look up and meet her gaze. A wordless exchange passed between them, and she held out the paper to Aletta.

"Thank you," Aletta whispered. "I'll look quickly."

"You can keep it," the young woman responded, unmistakable relief softening her voice.

With Andrew beside her, Aletta turned the pages, then scanned the list of names under the heading "Tennessee—Killed, Wounded, and Missing," all while telling herself she wasn't nurturing foolish hope.

She was simply still hoping.

CHAPTER 3

Aletta kept an eye on Andrew as she read through to the end of the list. No Warren Wesley Prescott. Under any category. No Richard Goodall either, although she did recognize two of the other names on the deceased list. Poor Virginia Cates and Margaret Kirby. Did the women even know the fates of their dear husbands yet?

She whispered a prayer for them, and a chilling wind swept it upward.

On the way home, she recalled a similar afternoon months earlier when she and Andrew had passed a contingent of Federal soldiers. As she'd looked into the eyes of the blue-clad enemy, she'd known she was looking into the eyes of some woman's husband, father, brother, or son. And as she'd contemplated many times before, she firmly believed that—given the chance—she could sit across the table from those women and together they could somehow chart a course to peace.

Peace that utterly eluded Generals Grant and Lee.

Why were men so drawn to war? It probably

revealed far too much about her, but she couldn't think of anyone or any political issue for which she would willingly sacrifice the lives of her children. Her own life? Perhaps. But those of her children? She couldn't fathom.

Later that night, after a dinner of leftover beans and corn bread, she tucked Andrew into bed on the straw mattress next to hers, then donned her shawl to fetch more wood for the fire. The night air was crisp, but at least the wind had subsided.

She stared up into the night sky pricked with stars, the quarter moon shining especially bright, and she wondered how much longer the war would continue. She smoothed a hand over her belly, not too surprised when the child within gave a tiny kick. "Patience, my love," she whispered. "Not quite yet."

A moment passed and she looked down, realizing she was doing it again—twirling the wedding band that was no longer there. She stared in the moonlight at the empty place on the ring finger of her left hand, knowing she'd made the right choice. She and Andrew had to eat, after all. It had been almost a year since she'd sold it to the jeweler in town, but still she felt naked without it.

Discovering how little wood was left in the bin, she retrieved the ax, situated a log atop the old oak stump, and brought the ax down with practiced force—something she wouldn't be able to do much longer. The log split clean down the middle. Since her parents had never had a son, she'd been forced to learn unusual skills for a woman. Skills that had proven helpful over the past two years since Warren had left. Not to say she hadn't missed Warren. She had, terribly. But she hadn't been quite so lost in certain ways as some of her friends had been.

She chopped wood until the bin was stocked for several more days, then, breath coming heavy, carried an armful into the house. The crackle of dry wood succumbing to flame filled the bedroom, and the warmth felt good on her skin.

She sighed and retrieved the newspaper, then settled into the chair by the fire to read. When she reached the editorial section, she felt herself tensing . . .

While the gentler sex is highly esteemed, it's clear they're best suited for hearth and home and utterly foolish to suggest that women should be involved in any way in the war effort. Their place is in rearing children and homemaking. And to insinuate that some females have managed to infiltrate the ranks of the army and are fighting alongside men even now is ludicrous. Not only would such women faint beneath the hardship of a soldier's life, they would flee in utter terror at the earliest sign of battle.

Aletta read on, not realizing until she'd read to the end of the letter how hard she was gritting her teeth. She consciously tried to relax her jaw as she scanned the letter written to the editor a second time, struck by her reaction to it while fully realizing the dichotomy of her thoughts.

Not that she herself ever wished to be in battle, not after the sights Warren had described with such agonizing detail. But that a man—the letter was simply signed "A soldier who loves his country"—would think so little of a woman's capacity as to limit her options to only "hearth and home." Was he not aware that women filled most of the factory jobs now? By necessity, yes. Because the men were off fighting. But still, females were doing the work and doing it quite well, from her perspective. She herself had worked briefly in a munitions factory, until the Federals took command of the town and shut it down. She huffed.

Such arrogance. Short-sightedness.

She turned the page, eager to move her thoughts to another subject, when a leaflet slipped from between the pages of newsprint and fluttered to the floor. She picked it up and read the ornately scripted banner across the top.

She scanned the printed handbill and softly read aloud, "A Christmas auction sponsored by the Women's Relief Society in support of our Confederate soldiers. Experienced cooks needed."

She lifted her gaze from the page, knowing precisely where she was going first thing in the morning.

"Are you questioning my order, Captain Winston?"

"No, sir, Colonel. I simply—" Jake read warning in the man's eyes and knew better than to try to bluff. Not after they'd been to the gates of Hades and back together. Yet he had to try to convince the senior officer. "Permission to speak freely, Colonel."

Seated behind his field desk, Stratton leaned back in his chair, cigar clamped between his teeth. "Lack of such has rarely stopped you before, Captain. But . . ." He gestured. "Permission granted. Speak your mind."

Jake hesitated as a bitter morning wind billowed the sides of the canvas tent, bringing with it a cold that sank clear through skin and straight to bone. He could scarcely feel his toes as it was. But at least he still had boots, what was left of them anyway. Which was more than most of the other soldiers could claim. He chose his words carefully.

"With all due respect, Colonel, I believe I can still be an asset here."

The colonel's smile came slowly. "You can believe anything you want, Captain. That doesn't change my order." He gave a throaty laugh. "I can't tell you how many soldiers would jump at a chance to get away from the front lines for a bit." He shook his head and all humor drained from his expression. "It's tough . . . what's happened to you, Captain, I know. You're one of the finest soldiers I've ever known. And the best sharpshooter this side of the Mississippi."

Jake stiffened, hearing a silent *were*—past tense—in the colonel's statement.

"There's no shame in what happened to you, Captain Winston. I've spoken to your commanding officer who was there at Chickamauga. There's nothing you could've done to prevent what happened."

Jake shook his head, seeing it all play out again in his mind's eye, feeling the bullet rip through his flesh seconds before his head struck the boulder. "I must have missed something, sir. Movement on the ridge, perhaps. Or maybe if I'd taken position a little farther to the east—"

"You didn't miss anything. One of their

42

sharpshooters finally got the jump on you that morning, that's all."

"And killed three of our officers."

"This is war, Captain Winston. Men die. And they'll keep on dying until the South puts an end to this conflict. Which I believe will be very soon. Meanwhile, you've got to find a way to move past Chickamauga."

"But how can I leave these men, sir? I can still serve here. I'm sure of it!"

"Part of what's at play here, Captain Winston, is that you've learned you're not invincible, no matter that your record up to now would reflect otherwise. You've all but single-handedly taken out the majority of the Federal's best sharp-shooters. Yet never once have you been seen, much less shot. Until now. Do you have any idea how many lives you've saved over the past two years?"

Jake held the colonel's stare but said nothing.

Stratton leaned forward in his chair, the joints creaking from the weight. "What's the doc's latest report?"

"He says my shoulder's healing fine, sir. Bullet went clean through. But he says I need to give it more time. That my long-range vision might come back. Or . . . it might not."

Stratton stared. "What does your gut tell you, soldier?"

Jake straightened. "That I'm ready for battle,

sir. Not like before, of course. But I can still shoot well enough to kill a Yankee."

"Is that so?" Colonel Stratton rose, his already imposing figure seeming more so in the confines of the tent. He laid aside his cigar and grabbed the rifle atop his trunk. "Follow me."

Outside, in the chill of early morning, dawn cloaked the encampment in a dusky purple gray as the sun edged its way up over the hills. Fog hung in ragged patches like tufts of cotton torn and scattered on the breeze. Jake followed, already knowing where the colonel was leading.

When they reached the target range, Stratton handed him the Whitworth and pointed. "Lowest limb of that poplar. Sixty feet out."

Mindful of the wound healing in his left shoulder, Jake brought the rifle close to his right, the movement as familiar to him as breathing. He lowered his head, feather-closed his left eye, and peered through the scope. Then blinked. Again and again. Despite the bone-chilling temperature, sweat slicked his skin. He squinted, concentrating. But no matter what he did, the world through the scope remained a distant blur.

"Take aim and shoot, Captain," Stratton commanded.

Jake's gut churned. He gritted his teeth. *Focus, focus!* Exasperated, he finally shook his head. "It's no good, sir," he whispered, his breath puffing white.

"You said you're ready for battle, soldier! That's a Yankee coming straight for you, sixty feet out. Except he's covering ground, and he's got a load of lead aimed straight at your heart. If he's slow and has some girth to him, that might give you a chance. But if he's fast and a fair shot, you're already dead. So take aim and fire, Captain."

"Sir, I said it's no good. I-I can't— "

"Take aim and *fire!*"

Jake squeezed the trigger and absorbed the familiar recoil of the rifle even as the sound of the bullet missing its mark caused something deep inside him to give way. An ache lodged in his chest and his eyes burned with emotion.

"Congratulations, Captain." Stratton clapped him on his good shoulder. "You're a dead man."

Stratton turned and strode back to his tent. After a moment, Jake did likewise, rifle in hand. He followed the colonel inside, returned the firearm to the trunk, and stood at attention before Stratton's desk, waiting to be dismissed. Stratton took his seat and said nothing. Just shuffled through papers, head down.

Moments passed.

Finally, the Colonel sighed. "Captain, you're obviously not ready to return to battle yet."

"But, Colonel, I—"

He raised a hand. "I spoke with the doctor, too, and he believes this assignment will be good for you. You need to rest your eyes, he says. Use those compresses and whatever other medicine he's given you. Doc says it'll speed the healing. If there's healing to be had," he added in a quieter voice. "And I concur with him that some time away from your regiment and the camp would do you good."

Jake looked at him. "Some *time,* sir? But we're scheduled to move out day after tomorrow, and I—"

"All the wounded are being transferred to Thompson's Station this afternoon. The convoy leaves at noon. Except for you." Stratton leveled his gaze. "General Bragg wrote asking for a special favor to an honorary colonel friend of his. That's where you come in."

Mention of General Bragg got Jake's attention.

Stratton eyed him. "It's a gathering of women, one of the Women's Relief Societies."

"A *Women's Relief Society,* sir?" Jake caught Stratton's frown and knew better than to interrupt again, their history and the permission to speak freely notwithstanding.

"They're hosting a fund-raiser for the Confederacy. It's being sponsored by some of Nashville's most prominent families, including General Bragg's cousin." Stratton picked up a letter from his desk. "The fund-raiser is being held at the home of a Colonel John McGavock of Carnton. Colonel McGavock's father was mayor of Nashville some time back. You heard of him? Or of Carnton?"

Jake shook his head. Had it really come to this for him? Looking after a bunch of petticoats?

"Carnton looks to be three or four miles south of here, down in Franklin." He pointed to the map lying open on his desk. "Seems *Mrs.* Colonel John McGavock, as she apparently prefers to be addressed, petitioned the higher-ups. She must have some pull with someone, too, because she sufficiently gained their attention. The letter is in General Bragg's own hand." Stratton began reading. " 'Mrs. Colonel John McGavock requests that we show our support for the Women's Relief Society as they show *their* continued support for the soldiers.' " Stratton looked up from the letter. "In short, Mrs. McGavock thinks that having a soldier in their midst would not only be an encouragement to the women, but also provide security for the event and the funds they'll be raising. But with the recent losses we've sustained"—Stratton tossed the letter aside—"I can't spare to send a man who has the ability to fight."

"So you're sending me . . . sir?"

Stratton smiled. "That's right, Captain. General Bragg expresses, and frankly, I agree, that sending a visibly wounded soldier—one of the amputees, for instance—would upset the ladies, make them more anxious about their men. But

47

your shoulder's healing, and you're healthy looking enough. And according to my wife, you're young and dashing." Sarcasm weighted the colonel's tone. "At least you might be . . . somewhere beneath all that growth of beard. And I imagine you can be sufficiently charming, when you put your mind to it."

Jake didn't share his humor. "Wouldn't it be easier, sir, just to tell the women to donate their money and valuables and be done with it? Would save us all a lot of time. After all, the gentler sex has no place in matters of war, sir. They're best shielded from war's cruelties. Better for them to stick to hearth and home."

Stratton smiled. "You sound like that letter to the editor I read yesterday."

"Sir?"

Stratton reached for the newspaper buried beneath the piles on his desk and pushed it toward him. "Fellow wrote in and lambasted the editor for suggesting that some women were actually fighting, even now, alongside the men. As if we wouldn't be able to tell the difference."

Jake unfolded the paper, found the editorial page, and scanned the letter.

"Next thing you know, Captain, they'll be saying we ought to allow women to hold command." Stratton laughed. "Can you imagine?"

Jake finally looked up and managed a smile. The wording in the letter was overly harsh, but he couldn't say he disagreed with the opinion overall. The way he looked at it, it wasn't so much that women lacked the constitution for war as it was that men had a God-bestowed duty to protect them from the horrors of it. He laid the paper aside.

"Back to your assignment at Carnton." Stratton reached for his partially smoked cigar, struck a match, and breathed new life into the tightly rolled tobacco leaves. Circles of smoke coiled upward. "We already know the Federals pulled out of Franklin some time back. Scouts confirmed this week that General Grant's army is advancing toward Mississippi while Rosecrans is pushing toward Chattanooga. There's a small garrison still holed up at Fort Granger, but they're keeping to that area. And word is, the fort has fallen into disrepair. We have Confederate troops quietly patrolling the area. Still, there's enough Federal rabble around to raise a ruckus, so best be on watch. And considering the money the women will be raising for the cause, having a soldier on the premises isn't a bad idea."

"Even one who can't see to shoot, sir?"

"I'm not sending you down there to kill Yankees, Captain. I'm sending you because you're not ready to fight again yet. I need you back here as soon as possible. The *Army* needs you back. But I need the man who moves like a ghost in the wind and hits his target from another world away. So keep to Carnton and to the town. And concentrate on healing up." His gaze sobered. "I trust you won't disappoint me *or* the General . . . Jake."

Jake shook his head, both humbled and resigned. "No, sir, Colonel. No disappointment. What are my duties while I'm there?"

Stratton puffed on the cigar, his smile coming slowly. "Whatever Mrs. Colonel John McGavock bids you to do. General Bragg also requests that something be written up about the Christmas event the women are hosting. You're good enough with a pencil. I've seen your sketches. Capture a scene or two that the newspaper can print and pen a few words to go with it. Come Christmas, it'll be published with a paragraph from General Bragg."

Jake simply nodded.

Stratton stood and rounded the desk, then moved toward the entrance of the tent, the canvas flap whipping in the wind. He nudged back the opening, and Jake stared past him out across the rippling tide of dingy-looking tents dotting the field as far as the eye could see, interrupted only by the occasional confiscated Federal soldier's tent, so prized among the men.

"Morale is low in the camps. You already know that," Stratton continued. "The men are worn down, short on hope, and they're worried about their families back home. So whatever scarves or gloves or knitted together whatnot you bring back from Carnton will be a boon to them, I'm sure. All Christmas furloughs are being canceled too. So when the men are told they won't be seeing their families, that won't help either. And despite the overall victory at Chickamauga, the losses at Vicksburg . . . and all that happened there . . . haunt us still."

At the mention of Vicksburg, Jake briefly bowed his head. He'd lost so much on that battlefield. Far more even than he'd lost at Chickamauga.

Stratton said nothing for a moment, then sighed. "Your fellow soldiers need to be reminded of why they're fighting, Captain. And of who they're fighting for. We could all use that reminder."

Jake heard fatigue in the colonel's voice.

Clearing his throat, Stratton turned back. "Captain Roland Jones from Captain P. R. Leigh's Company of Infantry, Mississippi Volunteers, should be here anytime to escort you to Carnton. Meet him on the main road south of camp. Godspeed, Captain. Dismissed."

Jake saluted, and Colonel Stratton returned the gesture.

"And, Captain . . ."

Jake turned.

"First chance, you might want to get a shave and a haircut. No need offending the ladies."

Jake managed a smile and hurried to his tent to grab his gear. He shoved his clothes into the knapsack along with his notebook and the spectacles the doctor had given him a few days earlier. He didn't like relying on the eyeglasses, but they did help him see close up when his eyes were tired, much as he didn't like to admit it. Knapsack slung over his good shoulder and haversack and rifle in hand, he quickly covered the distance to the road. Colonel Stratton was wrong about him needing time away for his sight to heal. It wasn't time away he needed. He needed to be back with his regiment, at least in some capacity, pushing the Federal Army farther north, sending them back where they belonged.

Not kowtowing to a bunch of crinolines.

CHAPTER 4

The near two-mile walk from the house to
Carnton felt much longer in the cold and wind,
and Aletta squeezed Andrew's little gloved hand
tucked inside hers. She sensed him watching
her and looked down to see him frowning, his
handsome little-boy face a more youthful image
of his father's.

"A penny for your thoughts, sweetheart?"

His brow furrowed. "I hear Santa Claus won't
be makin' it down here for Christmas, Mama.
Seth says it's 'cause of them good-for-nothin'
Yankees. Said they likely shot him to bits by
now. So there won't be any Christmas this year."

Aletta slowed. "When were you speaking with
Seth?"

"He came by yesterday while you was resting.
To bring back my ball."

Aletta gently pulled her son to the side of the
dirt drive and knelt to be at eye level with him.
She glanced toward the main house a short
distance away, hoping no one happened to be
peering out a front window. Here she was,
applying for the position of cook with a reference

letter praising her seamstress skills, which already didn't bode well. But arriving with a child in tow was another mark against her. Her breath ghosted white in the frigid morning air.

"I will remind you, Andrew, that you cannot take everything Seth says to heart. He's a good friend, but sometimes he spouts opinions upon subjects he knows nothing about." She coerced an unruly curl from his forehead, which promptly fell right back.

"So you're sayin' we *are* still havin' Christmas?" Andrew's dark brows knit together.

"Why . . . of course we are." Aletta hugged her son tight, needing to feel his arms around her neck as much as she needed for him not to glimpse her own sadness. She breathed in his little-boy scent before drawing back, her smile firmly in place. "I know it for truth that Santa is doing well. In fact, he's quite hearty from eating shortbread all year."

Andrew beamed. "Like the kind you used to make?"

She nodded. "However, from what I hear, he *will* be busy. More so than usual. Because there seem to be a lot more children who've been good, like you. So whatever he brings, however modest, Andrew, we must be grateful for it. Do you understand?"

He nodded, his impish smile widening. "When he brings me my red train engine, like Papa said,

I'll share it with anybody who wants to play with it!"

Aletta cringed, wishing for the thousandth time that Warren hadn't promised their son a train for Christmas while home on his furlough last April. She'd never be able to find such an extravagance, much less afford it. Not even if she managed to get this temporary job at Carnton. Because she still had the problem of where they were going to live in less than two weeks' time.

On the wind came the pungent scent of evergreen, and her gaze moved to the hills, to the leafless elm and poplar standing shoulder to shoulder with pine trees frocked in silvery winter green as though unwilling to be outdone. Where was God's hand of provision now, when she needed it most?

Bless her sweet son, he'd been four years old when he'd said good-bye to his papa when Warren left to fight. And now, two years later, she still wondered whether Andrew truly grasped that his papa wasn't ever coming home again. Andrew had wept the night she'd told him his papa had been killed and was now in heaven with Jesus and Grandpa and Grandma. But then days later he'd asked, yet again, when Papa would be home next.

"Your papa loves you very much," she whispered. "You know that."

He nodded.

"And while getting a train for Christmas would be very nice, we both need to remember that Christmas really isn't about *receiving* presents, is it?"

His gaze wary, he slowly shook his head.

She looked into his eyes. "It's about being thankful for the greatest gift God has ever given us."

He didn't respond.

"You know who that gift is, Andrew. He left heaven and came down to live among people just like us. He was born a baby and grew up to be a strong man, honest and true. Our Savior." She waited.

"Jesus," he finally whispered. "Who Papa's with."

Her eyes burned. "Yes, sweetie. Who Papa's with. Right now. And we'll both be with them, too, someday. But for now, you and Mama, we'll take care of each other as Jesus watches over us."

Andrew looked down. "And we'll take care of the baby too?"

She smiled. "Yes, and the baby too."

He framed her face in his palms and leaned close as though having a secret to tell. "I'll share my train from Papa with the baby," he whispered, then beamed.

Aletta had to smile, despite wondering if anything she'd said had truly registered.

She rose and smoothed a hand over the swell in her gray woolen skirt and noticed the singed hem toward the front. Wishing to hide the flaw, she cheated the waistband over to the side again and they walked on, hand in hand.

They reached the winter garden, and she spotted a line of carriages parked in front of the house, and hesitated. Carriages likely meant that Mrs. McGavock was hosting a gathering of some sort and the staff—and head cook—wouldn't appreciate being disturbed. But she'd come all this way. Too far to turn back now.

A bench drew her attention, nestled by a hedge of hydrangea near a towering osage orange tree. The bench, hidden from view of the house, was sheltered from the wind and would be a perfect place to wait unseen. She led Andrew into the natural alcove and immediately felt the difference in temperature minus the wintry gusts.

She motioned him toward the bench. "You wait here. I won't be long, sweetheart."

His cheeks ruddy with cold, he looked at the bench then at her and nodded. But the stubborn set to his jaw gave her pause.

She leaned down and tugged his coat collar closer about his neck. "Remember what we talked about. You must wait for me. Do not go exploring like you did the other day. This is a *very* important visit, and I need to—"

"How come I can't go too? Why do I have to

stay here? And how come I couldn't stay with Seth?"

Aletta hadn't even asked MaryNell if she would watch Andrew this morning. Not under the circumstances. She prayed again for MaryNell and for whatever decisions she faced. And prayed her friend would make the right ones.

"We've already been through why, Andrew. Mrs. Goodall was busy. Now I need you to stay here until I get back. Understood?"

He gave a begrudging nod, climbed up on the bench, then slumped down.

Aletta reached into her pocket and withdrew the folded napkin even as her own stomach growled. When he spotted the piece of bread and cheese she held out, he beamed.

"I thought you said we didn't have any extra!"

Aletta placed half of her breakfast in his outstretched palm. "You're a growing boy. And a growing boy needs nourishment."

He took a bite of bread then cheese, his jaw working furiously. It did her heart good to see him eat. The day she'd lost her job, she'd begun rationing what little was left in the pantry, stretching it to make it last. What few coins remained in her reticule would be enough for bread and another wedge of cheese and perhaps some milk, but after that . . .

She gave his hair a last tousle, then cut a path back to the gravel drive and around the fine carriages. She opened the front gate, a tree-lined serpentine-pattern brick walkway bridging the distance to the front portico. She made sure the gate closed behind her before continuing to the front entrance of the two-story redbrick home, fresh determination taking hold.

She would not leave here without a job.

She'd heard of Carnton and its owners, the McGavock family. What person living in Franklin, Tennessee, hadn't? But she'd never had cause to make the trek out here.

The estate encompassed a sprawling farm, and the main house—with its stately windows situated on the ground level and mirrored on the second—resembled a residence she'd once seen portrayed in *Harper's Weekly*. Never had she dreamed she'd actually set foot in such a place.

And she still might not, she reminded herself, if she couldn't talk her way into an interview.

The estate seemed awfully quiet for being so large. Not a worker in sight. But it was winter. And if Carnton was like other plantations, they'd sent their slaves south months ago, far from the reaches of Federal troops bent on freeing them.

She tugged her coat together in the front and climbed the stone steps to the portico, noting the detailed carpentry work of the four square columns supporting the upper porch. Her father had been a master carpenter, God rest him, and he'd bequeathed to her a considerable knowledge of woodworking, much to her late mother's dismay. Beveled recessed panels adorned each column, and a simple yet elegant vase-shaped balustrade enclosed both the lower and upper porches. Details that had lined some wood-worker's pocket quite nicely while adding considerably to the beauty of the home.

She'd never mastered carving but could build a solid, if simple, piece of furniture. She smiled remembering how Warren had teased her when he'd learned that the chest of drawers she brought to the marriage was one she'd crafted herself. "Land sakes, woman! If I'd known you could cook *and* build furniture, I'd have asked you to marry me sooner."

Sooner than two months? That was the length of time between when they met and when they married. Both of them had simply known. It helped that her parents had loved him like the son they'd never had.

A deep breath for courage, and she knocked on one of the paneled double doors. After a moment, she started to knock a second time, thinking perhaps—

The door opened. But no one was there. Or at least that's what she thought, until she looked down. A young boy peered up. About Andrew's age, she guessed, and with Andrew's slight build.

"May I help you, madam?" His serious tone

belied both his youth and the mischievous grin on his face.

Aletta swiftly decided to play along. "Yes, you may, kind sir." She curtsied and curbed a grin at the pleasure that lit his blue eyes. It felt good to be playful again, the way she and Andrew were, or used to be, together. Before the war, before Warren had gone away. "I'm here seeking an audience with the head cook," she continued. "If you would be so gracious as to inquire whether she has time to see me, I would be most grateful."

The boy blinked as if suddenly uncertain what to do next, then he straightened his shoulders and stepped to one side. "Please enter," he said stiffly, his chest puffing out.

Aletta did as he asked, half wondering if she should or not. After all, a child lacked the proper authority to invite guests into the home, and she didn't wish to jeopardize her chances for employment. Yet she needed to gain an audience with the cook if she hoped to get the job, which she wouldn't get standing out on the porch.

He closed the door behind her, and though the foyer lacked a hearth and was chilly, she welcomed protection from the wind—and hoped Andrew would stay where she'd left him.

"Wait here." The boy pointed to a certain section of floorcloth, and Aletta smiled and shifted slightly to the left to accommodate. He grinned, apparently pleased with her compliance, then disappeared through an open doorway to the right.

The thrum of female voices drifted through the closed door of one of the rooms farther down the hallway to the left, and she gathered that a meeting or some such was under way. A meeting involving a rather heated discussion, judging by the escalation of voices.

She waited. And waited. And began to feel more awkward as the moments lengthened. She peered out one of the sidelights, watching for any sign of Andrew, not putting it past him to—

"Miss Katharina Boudreaux?"

Startled, Aletta turned and found a woman staring at her.

The woman stepped closer. "You're the master pastry chef from Atlanta? We've been expecting you."

"Oh, no . . . I'm sorry." Aletta shook her head. "I'm not Miss Boudreaux. I'm . . . Mrs. Warren Prescott."

The woman's eyes narrowed. She scanned the foyer. "And pray tell, Mrs. Warren Prescott . . . precisely what are you doing standing in my front entrance hall? And who gave you entry?"

Hearing censure in the woman's tone, Aletta realized she'd made a serious misstep.

CHAPTER 5

Wishing now that she'd stayed outside, Aletta curtsied, certain she was addressing the mistress of Carnton. She only hoped her gaffe wouldn't cost her the position. "Hello, Mrs. McGavock. As I said, my name is Mrs. Prescott, and I'm here to interview for one of the positions as cook for the Women's Relief Society event. I've worked in a bakery before and certainly know my way around a kitchen. My mother was a head cook for the Parks family years ago, and she taught me well. And regarding how long I've been here . . . only a handful of moments, I give you my word. A young boy gave me entrance."

The uncertainty in the woman's countenance finally lessened by a degree. "Ah . . . that young man would be my son, Winder. He has taken to answering the door of late. And though I've instructed him to do otherwise, he is quite obstinate in his opinions for one so young."

Aletta offered a smile. "I could say the same of my own son, who I believe would be about your son's age."

The woman closed the distance between them.

"I'm Mrs. Colonel John McGavock. And while I appreciate your interest in the position, Mrs. Prescott—and your credentials—I'm sorry . . . All the positions for cooks have been filled. When the flyer first appeared in the newspaper earlier this week, we were deluged with applicants. I'm certain you can understand."

Hope deflated, Aletta tried not to let it show. "Of . . . of course, Mrs. McGavock. I didn't realize it had been advertised before yesterday." She felt a burning behind her eyes. "I don't suppose you have need of any other help? A housekeeper, perhaps? Or a laundry maid."

The woman eyed her. "I'm very sorry, but we don't."

Aletta nodded. "Well then, I won't take up any more of your valuable time. Good day, ma'am."

"Mrs. Prescott."

Hand on the doorknob, Aletta paused and looked back in time to see the woman's gaze drop briefly to her distended belly.

Mrs. McGavock's features softened. "It's particularly cold outside today. Perhaps you would like a cup of hot cocoa before your journey back to town?"

Thinking of Andrew, Aletta shook her head. "That's very kind of you, ma'am. But . . . I'd best not."

"But I insist, Mrs. Prescott. Come with me, and I'll show you to the kitchen."

Again, Aletta resisted. "I'm sorry, Mrs. McGavock, but—" She lowered her head. "My son is waiting for me outside. I didn't have anywhere else for him to stay this morning, so—"

"Well, that will not do at all! It's so cold! I'll have Winder invite him in straightaway. I wager your son would welcome a cup of hot cocoa as well." Mrs. McGavock strode to the door through which Winder had disappeared and opened it. "Winder, come quickly, please!" She glanced back to Aletta. "Your son's name, Mrs. Prescott?"

Aletta stared, near speechless at the woman's kindness. And her straightforward manner. "It's Andrew, ma'am. But truly, I don't—"

Winder appeared at the door, wearing the same mischievous grin from moments before, and Aletta began to wonder if that wasn't his usual countenance.

"Winder, dear. There's a boy about your age outside—" Mrs. McGavock looked back. "Where is he waiting, Mrs. Prescott?"

"On the bench in the garden, ma'am."

Mrs. McGavock nodded. "Winder, put on your coat and go fetch the young man and bring him inside for a cup of—"

Winder was out the front door and down the steps in a flash.

"Winder!" his mother called after him. "I

65

said put on your coat, young man!" She huffed beneath her breath as the boy ran full tilt toward the garden. "Boys are such rambunctious creatures. So different from girls."

"I'll have to take your word on that count, Mrs. McGavock." Aletta smiled.

The woman looked over, a sparkle in her eyes. "At least for now you will. But there may come a day in a few months when you'll know that fact for yourself only too well."

Aletta smoothed a hand over her rounded midsection. "Far sooner than that, I hope. January, I expect."

"So short a time remaining?" The woman's expression revealed her surprise. "I had assumed spring. But it's always more difficult to gauge with you petite women. I have a belly that size after eating a single petit four."

Aletta laughed softly, knowing she was jesting. Mrs. McGavock was a handsome woman with striking dark hair and pale skin. The dress she wore was finely tailored yet lacked the elaborate trappings of lace, silk, and pearls other women of similar wealth wore. Still, the manner in which Mrs. McGavock carried herself lent the gown simplistic elegance.

On first impression, the mistress of Carnton struck her as a most practical woman. And based on what Aletta had witnessed thus far, a woman not much concerned with what people thought of her, but rather concerned with people in general. Odd how such quiet humility encouraged such deep respect.

Aletta spotted Winder running back toward the house with Andrew fast on his heels, both boys grinning from ear to ear.

"Hot cocoa!" Winder cried as he bulleted across the threshold into the foyer.

Andrew echoed the call at the precise moment Aletta managed to catch him by the arm as he barreled past.

"Andrew!" Aletta held on when he tried to pull away, then gave him a swift look before turning him to face Mrs. McGavock. "Andrew, may I present Mrs. Colonel John McGavock, the lady of Carnton, and the kind woman who is offering you hot cocoa. Mrs. McGavock, my overly excited son"—Aletta winced playfully—"Andrew Thomas Prescott."

"You have hot cocoa?" Andrew asked, and Aletta grimaced.

As though anticipating Aletta's apology, Mrs. McGavock waved a hand. "Yes, we have cocoa, young man. And cookies too! Follow Winder there, and he'll show you to the kitchen."

The boys took off through the door on their right, yammering as they went, and Aletta followed Mrs. McGavock in their wake. They passed through what appeared to be the office for the estate.

Mrs. McGavock glanced back. "Your husband is fighting for the cause, Mrs. Prescott?"

"He was, ma'am." Aletta kept her voice soft. "I was notified of his death a month ago."

Mrs. McGavock paused beside an open door that led to two sets of stairs, one set leading up to the second story and the other down to the kitchen, judging by the savory aromas wafting toward them. Genuine concern shadowed her expression. "I'm so sorry, Mrs. Prescott. My heart goes out to you in your loss. And that of your son of his father."

Aletta nodded, briefly bowing her head. "Thank you, ma'am. And your husband, Mrs. McGavock? Is he fighting?"

"Colonel McGavock is of some years now, so he was not called into service. Though he does support the effort in many ways. His title is honorary in nature, but is nonetheless important to him."

"To you both, I'm sure."

Mrs. McGavock nodded, sadness creeping into her expression. "Even so, the war has touched us deeply. My brother, Felix Grundy Winder, fell at Vicksburg this past summer. There are days I still find it difficult to grasp that he's truly gone from us."

Hearing the pain in her voice, Aletta remembered Warren writing her about the battles at Vicksburg and how many had died there. Over seven thousand killed or wounded, if memory served. The confrontation at Vicksburg had given new meaning to the cruelty of warfare. "I'm so sorry for your loss, Mrs. McGavock. So many, too many, have died."

Her hostess nodded then continued down the stairs and into a spacious kitchen that boasted an enormous hearth with a fire blazing brightly. An older Negro woman stood before a cast iron stove stirring a large pot, the comforting aroma hinting at potatoes and onions and a plentiful cupboard.

Aletta considered herself diminutive, but this woman was even more so. Scarcely four feet tall, she estimated, and that included the shock of gray hair caught up in a kerchief on her head. Yet the woman lifted a large cast iron kettle from the stove without the least sign of strain and poured a measure of its steaming contents into two over-sized mugs.

No delicate china teacups for the two boys seated at a table by the window, eager-eyed and watchful as they devoured a plate of what appeared to be butter cookies. Her own stomach complaining from want, Aletta took comfort in knowing that Andrew would talk about this for days on end.

"Tempy, this is Mrs. Prescott who came inquiring about the positions for cook. I told her they've been filled, but I invited her to enjoy a cup of cocoa before she starts back home."

"Yes, ma'am, comin' right up. You want some, too, Missus McGavock?" The older woman reached for another cup.

"None for me, Tempy, thank you. I must return to my meeting in the family parlor before a skirmish breaks out."

Tempy's high, airy laugh sounded like the tinkling of a bell. "Missus Tyler gettin' outta sorts 'bout my bread puddin' again? If I'd known that's what the lady wanted for dessert today, I coulda made it."

"No, it's not about the bread pudding. As serious an issue as that is . . ."

Aletta caught the humorous look that passed between the two women.

"It's actually about something pertaining to the auction." Mrs. McGavock included Aletta with a glance. "The Women's Relief Society hired an older gentleman to build a booth and manger for a life-sized nativity scene. You know him, Tempy. It's Mr. Baker."

"Kind old soul, that Mr. Baker." Tempy set a cup of cocoa on the worktable between them and aimed a smile at Aletta.

"Thank you," Aletta said softly, her interest more than a little piqued by the conversation. She wrapped her hands around the mug, the warmth causing a shiver. And as she sipped, she realized she'd all but forgotten this sweet, smooth, chocolatey delight.

"Yes, Mr. Baker is a kind old soul. It was our thought that the children could take turns being Joseph and Mary, as it were. But Mr. Baker has had to withdraw his offer due to his rheumatism. With the rest of the slaves sent away, and the Colonel busy with the farm, I can't think of anyone else to ask either. Neither can the other members of the committee. And the women are divided amongst themselves. Half are saying we don't need the nativity scene and the other half are saying we can't have the auction without it. I, for one, believe the Lord will understand us not having a booth and a manger for him. But not helping the soldiers as best we can with what we have?" Mrs. McGavock shook her head. "Not while I'm serving as committee chair. Still . . . it's a pity we can't find anyone else to make the items. The children would have enjoyed it so, and it would have been a tangible reminder for them, and the adults, of who lies at the heart of every effort behind this event."

Aletta set her mug on the table. "Mrs. McGavock, I know this may sound forward of me, and I certainly don't mean to come across that way. But . . . my father was a master carpenter, and he taught me a great deal about woodworking." Already, she could glimpse the thoughts forming in Mrs. McGavock's mind. "I realize it's not a typical skill for a woman, but

71

I'm certain I would know how to build whatever you're imagining for the nativity scene. All I would need is someone to help me lift the pieces and put it together. And I'd be happy to do the work for whatever you're able to pay." She felt her face heat. "I truly am in need of a job."

Mrs. McGavock took her time in responding. "Mrs. Prescott," she finally said, her voice gentle. "I appreciate what you're offering, and admire your tenacity. And while I believe women can do a great many things not customarily attributed to our gender, I do not believe a woman in . . . the family way"—she spoke the words softly—"could, or even should, strive to undertake such a task. I fear it would put at risk both your health and that of your child."

"Don't let my stature mislead you, Mrs. McGavock. I'm quite strong and able to do the work, I promise you. And with no threat to my child. I would never do anything to harm him. Or her," she added with a smile, recalling their earlier exchange.

Mrs. McGavock eyed her, then sighed. "You're most persuasive, Mrs. Prescott. And I would say yes"—the woman lifted a hand—"if not for the fact that there is no 'someone' here to help you in that regard. Tempy already has more work than one woman can do. And with the pastry chef arriving anytime now, and cooking not only for the auction and those food sales, but for the women volunteering to knit and sew for the soldiers beforehand . . . her load is only going to increase. So I fear that we shall simply have to make do with the two small crèches we have. We'll display them on the front table in the foyer and by the Christmas tree. But thank you, Mrs. Prescott, most sincerely, for your offer. Now, if you'll excuse me, I must force myself back into the fray. Please stay and enjoy your hot cocoa."

And with that, Mrs. McGavock turned to leave. Aletta felt her face fall.

"Oh, and, Tempy," Mrs. McGavock said. "The soldier Colonel Stratton is sending to help with the auction should arrive sometime today. The colonel said he's one of the wounded. So please see to him and make certain he has whatever he needs in the house out back."

"Yes, ma'am. I'll do that."

Aletta watched Mrs. McGavock go, feeling as though the woman were taking her last hope with her. Her gaze fell to Andrew and Winder, both boys quiet, momentarily under the spell of warm cocoa and cookies.

"You really know how to do all that, ma'am? With the wood?"

Aletta looked back to find Tempy watching her, her expression questioning.

"Yes. My father never had a son to teach,

so"—she lifted her shoulders and let them fall—
"he taught me instead. I enjoy it. Woodworking
is . . . gratifying. Even comforting."

Tempy shook her head. "A lady carpenter. I
ain't never heard of that before."

"And I've never had hot cocoa this delicious
before."

"Well then, let me fill your cup again."

Tempy offered her a cookie as well, and Aletta
accepted, eating it far too quickly, she knew.
But it tasted so good, and she was hungry. And
she'd been right. Butter cookies. One of her
favorites.

"Oh!" Tempy scowled. "Look what I gone and
done. Put too much pepper in the soup. What was
I thinkin'?" She exhaled, tiny hand on hip. "Here,
you taste it, Missus Prescott. Tell me if you think
it's still fit for eatin'."

Tempy ladled a generous portion into a cup and
set it before Aletta, who saw precisely what the
woman was doing. At another time in her life she
might've politely declined. But not today.

Aletta lifted the cup to her lips and sipped.
Then briefly closed her eyes. Potato soup, with
bits of bacon. "It's divine. Too much pepper
and all." She slipped the woman a grateful look,
which earned her a grin.

She sipped for a moment while Tempy worked,
then looked over to see the boys whispering in
hushed tones, the spell of warm cookies and

cocoa apparently fading. They jumped up.

"Mama, can I go with Winder to the barn? He says there's kittens!"

"Andrew, we need to leave shortly and—"

"Please?" he added, only to have Winder repeat it.

Aletta glanced out the window, then heard Tempy's soft whisper behind her. "Barn's out back. Only just out that door, ma'am. You could 'bout watch him from where you sit."

Aletta nodded. "All right. Go. But wear your coats. Both of you!"

"Yes, ma'am!" they said in unison and darted back out the kitchen the way they'd come.

A moment later, Aletta spotted the boys outside, racing for the barn, coats on but unbuttoned. She shook her head.

"It's only you and your boy then, Missus Prescott? With your husband away at war?"

Aletta looked back to see Tempy stirring the soup. "Actually, it's only Andrew and me." She glanced down. "And this little one, of course. Warren, my husband, was killed. Earlier this fall."

Tempy shook her head. "One of the hardest things in this life . . . losin' those we love. Havin' to go on without 'em."

A depth of empathy colored the woman's tone, a kindred kind of loss that went far beyond the simple offering of a condolence, and Aletta

75

found herself unable to offer a reply. Death had taken Warren from her. But Aletta knew that Tempy, as a slave, had no doubt suffered losses stemming from death, and far worse. Because in many cases, for a slave, the person you loved hadn't died. They'd been bartered or sold as though they weren't human, flesh and blood like everyone else. Mothers sold away from children, children from fathers and mothers, families torn asunder.

At least she knew where Warren was, even if she wished he were still here.

"When you expectin' that baby, Missus Prescott?"

Pulling her thoughts back, Aletta managed a smile. "Toward the end of January."

The woman smiled. "It's a blessed child who's carried close to a mother's heart through Christmastime. Soakin' up all that love and goodness."

Considering her current circumstances, Aletta wasn't too certain about that, but hoped her expression didn't convey her doubt. "Tempy . . . That's a unique name."

The woman smiled. "My mother give it to me when I's just a girl. Not meanin' to, I guess. She always said I had me a temper, and she used to warn me about it, too, sayin', 'Careful now, Cecelia. Temper, temper!' Somehow my younger brother and sister never got good enough hold of my front name. So I guess they latched onto what they could."

Aletta studied her. "You don't strike me as the kind of person who would have a temper."

The old woman shook her head. "Well, life has a way of smoothin' out the rough edges of a person. Of takin' what seems so all-fired important and showin' you its real face. No, it's been years since that young girl looked out through these old eyes, but I swanny"—her expression grew thoughtful, even melancholy—"if there aren't times when I can't still feel herself livin' and breathin' inside me."

Aletta nodded thoughtfully. She'd be twenty and five on her next birthday come spring, yet felt twice that most days, and caught only occasional glimpses of the youthful bride she'd been a short lifetime ago. Yet she told herself not to give up hope. The newspapers wrote of the war ending soon and of the South's pending victory. Oh, she prayed that would be true. Though the prediction was based on newspaper accounts, she found herself doubting it, the Federal Army so much larger as a whole and better equipped than the Confederate.

Yet love for home and family and the determination to have a voice in the law of the land had to count for something too. She and Warren had never owned slaves. Neither had their parents nor most of the people they knew.

That hadn't been at the heart of this conflict for them. How many nights had she and Warren stayed awake late discussing this, most heatedly, before he'd left to join the Tennessee Army.

"This isn't only about slavery, Aletta. President Lincoln refuses to recognize the Confederate States of America. He sent a garrison to occupy Fort Sumter! The Confederates attempted to negotiate their withdrawal, but again, Lincoln refused. Now he's issued a call-up for seventy-five thousand troops to put down what he's terming 'the rebellion' in the South. We have a president claiming power for himself—and the government—that *far* exceeds what's given to him by the Constitution. And if we don't stand up now, I fear that what was fought for almost a hundred years ago might be lost forever."

Aletta stared into the empty mug of cocoa, once again acknowledging Warren's fear even as her original fear crowded her own heart. That fighting this war—however true and noble the variety of reasons—would, in the end, prove far too costly. To both sides.

She watched Tempy kneading a mound of bread dough on a stone worktable, the yeasty aroma filling the kitchen, and she wondered at the woman's past. And her future. Her movements were almost hypnotizing in the warmth and coziness of the kitchen, and Aletta sighed within herself. If only she'd responded to the ad sooner.

She rose, mindful of not overstaying her welcome. "Thank you, Tempy, for your kindness. Both to me and my son."

"Oh, ma'am, no trouble at all. I hope you find a place to plant yourself real soon." Warmth deepened the brown of her eyes, and Aletta smiled.

"I do too. I'll still come back and offer what help I can around the time of the auction, if I'm able. I'd like to be a part of it."

Footsteps sounded on the stairs and Aletta turned to see a woman who looked every bit a soldier on a mission.

"Tempy, I'm looking for—" The woman stopped, her attention falling on Aletta. "Oh, forgive me. I didn't mean to intrude."

"On the contrary." Aletta offered a smile. "I was taking my leave."

The woman nodded. "I don't suppose either of you have seen Master Winder anywhere about. He was supposed to return to the classroom by now."

Tempy laughed. "He's in the barn, Miss Clouston. Holdin' school with some kittens."

"In the barn?" The woman exhaled.

Aletta stepped forward. "I fear my own son may be partially to blame for leading him astray. I'll go get the boys immediately."

Miss Clouston shook her head. "Winder needs no help in that department, I assure you. The boy is intelligent beyond his years, but his attention is like that of a puppy come spring! Which is constantly getting him into trouble." She laughed softly. "I'm Elizabeth Clouston, the children's nanny."

Aletta liked her smile, so natural, genuine. "I'm Aletta Prescott. I came today in reference to the advertisement for cooks. But it seems I was too late."

"I'm sorry to hear that."

"Me too," Tempy said behind her, and they all laughed.

Aletta slipped her coat on. "I'm going to the barn now. I'll send Master Winder back to you."

"That would be much appreciated. It was a pleasure to meet you, Mrs. Prescott."

"You as well, Miss Clouston."

Already missing the warmth and welcome of this household, Aletta let herself out the front door of the kitchen and was met by a stiff northern wind—and the unmistakable scent of snow. She peered up and hoped she and Andrew could get back to town before the gray skies unleashed their threat.

Pulling her coat closer about her expanding middle, she started around the house toward the barn in the back when she noticed another carriage parked behind the others, and a woman exiting with the assistance of the driver. The woman stood for a moment staring up at the house before continuing toward the front door. Judging by her slight frown, Aletta assumed she wasn't overly impressed.

The *master* pastry chef, Aletta assumed, remembering what Mrs. McGavock had said. Yet this young woman looked far too youthful to have achieved that status. Still . . .

She'd read in *Godey's* of a wealthy young woman who had eschewed marriage and gone abroad to study cooking and baking and then returned to the States—New York City, if she remembered correctly—to open up her own bakery, or *patisserie* as the article had called it. She couldn't imagine having the wherewithal to do that. She didn't hail from a wealthy family, after all. And traveling so far from home . . . She'd never traveled outside Tennessee. Nor wanted to. This was her home.

She hurried to the barn, eager to escape the cold and wind, when she spotted yet another conveyance coming up the road. Even from a distance, she recognized the familiar gray of the two uniformed men riding in a buckboard. The wounded soldier Mrs. McGavock had mentioned.

Poor man. Likely an amputee like the former soldier she'd seen days earlier. Life was hard everywhere she looked. Which made her more determined to be grateful for what she did have, even if gratitude wasn't her natural response at present.

Feeling the not-so-gentle movements of the child inside her, she hurried into the barn just as the first flurries of snow began to fall.

CHAPTER 6

"I'm glad I was the one asked to bring you out here, Captain Winston. After hearing all those stories about you, me and the others had begun to think you weren't real."

"Oh, I'm real all right, Captain Jones." Jake glanced at the fellow officer seated beside him on the wagon bench. "Although I doubt all the stories you've heard about me are. They tend to grow a mite in the retelling."

Reins in hand, Jones laughed. "Maybe. But you're somewhat of a legend to the rest of us sharpshooters. Which made hearing about what happened to you even harder to take in. Getting shot in the shoulder was bad enough, of course. But the other . . ." He shook his head. "Sure hope you heal up all right."

"Thank you, Captain." Jake turned his coat collar up against the wind and snow.

He'd been surprised when, earlier, Jones had told him that his being wounded was a topic of conversation among some of the men. And while he appreciated the captain's well wishes, Jake felt uncomfortable. Such praise had never bothered him before. But now it only served to remind him of his temporary loss.

At least he hoped it was only temporary.

"You're from Mississippi?" Jake asked. "I think that's what the colonel said."

Jones nodded. "Town of Yalobusha. Born and raised there. You?"

"South Carolina."

"A low-country man."

Jake smiled.

"You got a family, Winston?"

"Nope." Jake shook his head. "You?"

Jones didn't answer for a moment. "I did. My wife and daughter died earlier this year. A few days apart."

Jake looked at him. "I'm so sorry."

His focus ahead, Jones nodded, then sighed. "Here I am in a war, and they die back at home. Doesn't seem quite fair now, does it?"

"No," Jake said quietly. "It doesn't."

As they passed a grove of pecan trees, Jake thought of the pecan pies his mother used to make, all sweet and buttery, especially just pulled from the oven, the pecans on top crusted with syrup. Best he'd ever had. Maybe it was seeing all the homes on his way to Franklin from the encampment, but he felt a measure of home-sickness he couldn't quite account for. His grip tightened on his rifle.

With both parents gone and Vicksburg having

robbed him of what precious family had remained, there was nothing left for him back in South Carolina now. The family farm, modest even at its height, was gone to ruin. Only memories lingered now. Of good times, mostly. At least those were the ones he tried to nurture.

Jones guided the wagon to a stop behind a line of carriages parked in front of the house—quite the busy place—and set the brake. Haversack and rifle in hand, Jake climbed down.

"Thanks again for the ride, Captain Jones."

"My honor, Captain Winston."

To Jake's surprise, Jones saluted, something not required of officers of equal rank.

Jake returned it, then retrieved his knapsack from beneath the bench seat. The still-tender wound in his left shoulder pulsed a bit, and he paused until the pain subsided, looking back at the house again. So this was Carnton.

If the McGavocks' home wasn't impressive enough, the acreage was. The gently rolling hills of evergreen, poplar, and pine. Cattle dotting the fields soon to be covered in snow. He'd seen sheep and hog pens in the distance and wondered if the McGavocks had had their hog killing yet. What with the freezing temperatures setting in, now would be the time if they hadn't.

Jones crossed to a door located on the right wing of the house, and a black woman answered. Jake couldn't overhear their exchange, but the

85

woman nodded. Captain Jones returned and began untying the tarpaulin that secured the wagon bed. Jones pulled back the cover to reveal a load of supplies and hefted a large crate to his shoulder.

Seeing the amount of work ahead and with the wind and snow picking up, Jake set aside his gear and picked up a medium-sized crate—and immediately realized he'd underestimated its weight. What was in here? Cannonballs? He quickly shifted the weight toward his right arm. And call it pride, but he wasn't about to set the box back down.

The captain paused and looked over at him.

Jake met his gaze. "I'm wounded, Jones. Not dead."

The hint of a smile showed on Jones's face as he walked on.

Jake deposited his box inside the kitchen door and caught a whiff of something that caused his stomach to rumble. Only then did he see the word *Flour* stamped on the side of the crate he'd just carried. A wagonload of kitchen staples? That's what Jones had brought? Jake thought again of how much more sense it made for these women to simply donate their money directly to the cause instead of throwing parties for each other in an effort to raise funds.

Frustrated all over again at this assignment, he retraced his steps to the wagon, feeling muscles he hadn't used in a while. The snow began to let up a bit even as the air seemed to grow colder.

A holler drew his attention and he turned to see two young boys racing for all they were worth around the corner of the house and toward the front gate. Time seemed to bend back on itself and he saw himself and young Freddie racing through the fields back home. Could feel the gentle whip of winter grasses as the two of them vied for a swift path of victory, Pa driving the wagon some distance behind them, the dinner bell urging them on. And Mother standing on the front porch watching for them all.

Jake swallowed at the vivid memory and took a deep breath, willing the emotion within him to subside as he pulled the memory closer, not wanting to lose hold of it. Or of them. Why the sudden tide of reminiscence, he couldn't say. Time of year, he guessed. He'd always liked Christmas. Had looked forward to it in years past. But this year the approaching holiday had an empty feel to it, and he wished it were already past.

One of the boys opened up the gate and shot up the walkway and into the house, while the other lingered at the edge of the fence as the gate slammed shut on him.

"Andrew!"

Jake turned at the voice and saw a woman walking hurriedly in that direction. Her near ankle-length coat hid the precise definition of her figure, but he was fairly certain she was with child. As if sensing his attention, she looked his way. He smiled, and she acknowledged him with a brief but polite tilt of her head.

"Andrew, come quickly." She gestured. "We need to start back to town."

"But I don't wanna leave, Mama! I like it here!"

She joined the boy and spoke in low tones, turning her back to the wagon.

Taking the hint, Jake picked up another crate, this one slightly smaller than the first but—as he swiftly found out—even heavier. He angled the crate and saw the word *Sugar* stamped on the side, and his frustration only deepened. No telling how much the contents of this crate alone cost. And like so many other soldiers, he hadn't tasted sugar in two lifetimes.

"You take *all* my friends away!" the boy yelled.

Jake couldn't help but look back. The mother knelt and drew her son to her as he cried, but the boy tried to push away. Finally, Andrew— Jake thought that was the name she'd used— relinquished his struggle and slipped his arms around her neck. Judging by the gentle shudder of her own shoulders, she was crying now too.

Jake carried the crate on to the kitchen, passing Jones along the way, the captain having missed the exchange by the front gate. Jake set his box down inside the door and returned to find the woman wiping her son's face and whispering something soft and sweet sounding.

The boy nodded, then sniffed and wiped his nose on his coat sleeve, an act Jake figured usually earned him an admonishment. But not in that moment.

The woman finally rose and dabbed at her own cheeks, then held out her hand. The boy looked up, such love yet such consternation in his expression that Jake wished he could sketch the image right then, capture a snippet of the power a mother's love held over a little boy's heart. A love he knew only too well. One that had grown and matured through the years, to be certain. But a love he still missed every day of his life.

The boy slipped his hand into hers, and Jake felt something joggle his memory.

"Ma'am? May I have a word with you, please?"

She turned, wiping the corners of her eyes. Eyes that held a question, and that were the prettiest shade of blue he could ever remember seeing. She nodded.

"I overheard you say just now, ma'am, that you need to head back to town. I happen to know from an earlier conversation with Captain Jones there"—he motioned to Jones, who stood in the doorway speaking with the black woman— "that's he's heading back that way. I'm certain

89

he'd welcome the chance to give you and your boy a ride, if you like."

"You mean we could ride in a real army wagon?" The boy's eyes went wide.

Jake smiled. "With real army horses."

The boy looked up at his mother, who offered a smile she couldn't quite hold.

"We'd be grateful, Mr. . . ."

"Captain Winston, ma'am."

"Thank you, Captain Winston. I'm Mrs. Warren Prescott. And this is my son, Andrew."

Jake gave the boy a salute and smiled when Andrew puffed out his chest and gave one right back.

"I'll talk to the captain right now. Let him know." Jake grabbed another crate and spoke with Jones at the house, then returned. "You're all set, Mrs. Prescott."

"Thank you, Captain." But something in her expression had changed, something he couldn't define. She walked closer, son in hand. "You're the wounded soldier, the one Mrs. McGavock said was arriving today?"

Jake hesitated. "Yes, ma'am. That's right."

Her gaze went to the crates in the wagon bed, then back to him.

"Captain, I have a question to ask you. One that will sound strange, I realize. But if a person was to request your help in building a simple nativity—a booth and a manger—would you

90

be able to lend assistance? To hold the pieces together and such?"

For an instant, he wondered if the woman was here by Colonel Stratton's design, a spy, of sorts, to see if he was truly going to *rest* like the doctor ordered. Then he smiled, realizing she had to be asking for her son's sake. Maybe the boy wanted to build a nativity for under the Christmas tree. "Yes, ma'am. I reckon I could do that."

A smile the likes of which he hadn't seen in far too long swept her face, and her eyes glistened. "Thank you, Captain." She whispered something to her boy, then looked back. "Would you mind if Andrew waited here with you for a moment while I go back inside? I won't be long."

"Take your time, Mrs. Prescott. Your son looks pretty strong there. I'm betting he could help us carry some crates."

The boy's eyes lit as he ran over. Jake hefted another crate and Andrew followed along, pushing up on the bottom from beneath, his slender jaw firming with the effort.

True to her word, Mrs. Prescott returned minutes later just as he and Andrew returned from unloading the last crate. If Jake hadn't known better, he might've thought she wanted to hug him.

"Thank you again, Captain Winston, for agreeing to help me. This means a great deal to me. And to Andrew as well."

Jake nodded. She was a delicate-looking woman. And pretty, with dark hair and eyes so deep a blue that, close up, they looked almost violet. And she was most decidedly with child, now that he got a closer look. And married. Mrs. *Warren* Prescott, she'd made a point of saying. Lucky man, that Warren Prescott.

"You're welcome, ma'am. I should be here for a few days, so just let me know when you need the help."

"Oh, I will, Captain. I will."

He assisted her into the wagon, the feel of her hand soft and silky in his. Even after letting go of her, her lingering warmth stayed with him, as did her indescribable sense of womanliness that threatened to rob him of thought even as it brought him to attention. He lifted Andrew up beside her and the boy settled himself between her and the captain. Jake walked as far as the front porch before he turned to watch the wagon as it disappeared in the swirl of wind and snow.

CHAPTER 7

Jake stood to one side in the entrance hall as a delegation of women left the house in a flurry of conversation about a coming winter storm, an intense loathing of having to miss someone's potato soup, and someone's displeasure over the lack of bread pudding. And again he wished he could thank Colonel Stratton for assigning him to this event.

He took in the niceties of the entrance hall—the expensive-looking cream and black diamond floorcloth, carpeted staircase, a handsome archway that accented the space, and the papered walls. Definitely a family of means, even in the midst of a war. At last, his hostess—whom he'd met only briefly before the mass exodus—rejoined him.

He again offered a slight bow. "Mrs. Colonel John McGavock . . . I take it that was the Women's Relief Society?"

"Oh gracious no, Captain Winston. That's only the committee. There are well over two hundred of us in the society."

Colonel Stratton's smirk came so clearly to his mind.

"And all of us, but especially the committee, are most appreciative to General Bragg for his willingness to lend your services to our event. We seek to raise money for the cause, of course. But also, and perhaps even more importantly, we seek to raise the spirits of the men who are fighting, as well as those of their families who wait most earnestly for their return."

"I can assure you, ma'am, the men are equally ready to return home. Victorious, of course."

Her smile dimmed by a fraction. "Of course, Captain. That is what we all hope. But *returning* is what is foremost in the hearts and minds of the women and children. Now please . . . if you'll follow me."

She led him through a door on the left and into a front parlor. He waited for her to take a seat then did likewise.

"Would you care for a cup of tea, Captain?"

"Yes, please." It had been so long since Jake had been asked that question, since he'd been in such a civilized setting, that the delicate pastel-colored porcelain cup and saucer felt awkward in his grip. "Thank you, ma'am."

The tea was hot and strong, the way he liked it, and smelled faintly of cloves and cinnamon, tastes he'd all but forgotten. Which made the savoring even more enjoyable.

"Colonel McGavock is presently working the farm, Captain. But he's eager to meet you as well. So I hope you'll join us for supper this evening, as you're welcome to do every evening you're here at Carnton. That will give us the opportunity to introduce you to our children, Hattie, our eldest, and Winder, her younger brother."

"I'd like that very much. Thank you, Mrs. McGavock."

He listened, nodding on occasion as she shared her expectations and goals for the auction and his duties accordingly. Which basically boiled down to what Colonel Stratton had told him— anything Mrs. Colonel John McGavock requested he do.

"In the midst of my appreciation for your presence here, Captain, I am very much aware that you, too, are a wounded soldier, and that you need your rest. So while you're here at Carnton, I'll depend upon you to set your limits and then communicate them to me. I have been known to ask a great deal of others." A smile hinted at the corners of her mouth. "Though, granted, nothing beyond what I expect of myself."

Jake nodded, completely believing her admission.

"Speaking of," she continued, "you're certain you're able to assist Mrs. Prescott in her . . . undertaking? She told me you very graciously agreed to help her."

"Oh yes, ma'am. I'm happy to help with the nativity."

"Very good then. The funds raised by our auction will be used to benefit the soldiers directly, a portion of which will be designated specifically for those wounded. A man who has fought for his country and who is left challenged in that regard deserves all the assistance we can offer him."

"That's most kind of you, Mrs. McGavock."

"Very good then." She rose. "If you're finished with your tea, allow me to see you to the kitchen. And Tempy, Carnton's head cook, will show you where you'll be staying while you're here. Did your commander tell you, by chance?"

He set his empty cup and saucer on the silver tray and followed her across the hallway and into what appeared to be an office. "No, ma'am, he didn't. But I'm assuming in the barn, which will be fine."

"Oh gracious no, Captain. We can do much better than that." She paused. "We have a cabin for you. Granted, it's one of the slaves' quarters. But it's by far the nicest. It's the brick cabin just beyond the kitchen and smokehouse where the house slaves resided. Those will be your private quarters, Captain, and you're to advise Tempy should you have need of anything."

Jake nodded. "Thank you, ma'am."

"I apologize that we're unable to host you in our home. But my own dear mother will be visiting soon as well as a cousin. So I fear the guest room is in high demand."

"The cabin will be more than fine, ma'am. Thank you. By chance, has Carnton had its hog killing yet?"

"No, we haven't. In fact, I believe the Colonel is planning to hold that in the next couple of weeks."

"I've butchered plenty of hogs back on the farm in South Carolina. Every winter since I was a boy. I'd be happy to help, if you'd like."

Her eyes brightened. "I'm sure the Colonel would be happy to have your assistance, Captain. As with other farms, all of our slaves but one, Tempy, the head cook I've mentioned, have been sent south. So every hand is a welcome addition to the work." She continued on toward a doorway that led to two sets of stairs. One leading up to the second story and the other leading down. "I meant to inquire earlier, Captain . . . Have you taken your noonday meal yet?"

"No, ma'am, I haven't."

"Then we'll remedy that straightaway. Tempy is the best cook in all of Tennessee. She's been with us for years now. And I'm certain she'll have something you'll—"

"I *must* have my kitchen worktables scrubbed clean!" A strident female voice carried toward them from around the corner. "And we *must* have a table dedicated solely for working pastry dough. That is imperative. Every experienced chef knows this. This one here will do." A rapping noise followed. "Once it's properly cleaned, of course. Get to it immediately. And no other food is to touch it. Is that understood?"

"Yes, ma'am," came a quiet voice.

"Yes, ma'am?"

"Yes, ma'am . . . *Chef Boudreaux.*"

Mrs. McGavock exhaled, her expression darkening. She descended the short staircase, and Jake followed, his curiosity more than a little roused.

"Miss Boudreaux." Mrs. McGavock's tone was polite yet had gained an edge. "I trust you're getting settled into Tempy's kitchen."

Jake didn't miss the emphasis on ownership, nor the tiny black woman he'd seen at the door a while earlier whose eyes were downcast. But the young woman who turned to face them, she was new.

Her white-blond hair was piled high in a chaos of tight curls and her hands were fisted at her waist. She smiled and her expression lost a degree of its censure, though not enough to cover the fire in her eyes or her demeanor that reeked of disapproval.

"Yes, Mrs. McGavock, I am. Though I am finding the conditions considerably more . . .

rustic than I was led to believe. But I'm certain I can still work here. After all—"

She tossed Jake a look that he thought she meant to be coy and perhaps even alluring. It had the exact opposite effect.

"—I am Katharina Boudreaux, a professional chef trained in Paris."

Mrs. McGavock smiled, yet Jake felt the air crackle with warning, much like the moment before a battle ensued.

"Yes, Miss Boudreaux, I'm aware of your accomplished résumé. Mrs. Tyler presented it to the committee when she insisted we hire you. However, Mrs. Tyler did not share that you would denigrate a trusted and beloved servant in this household. Nor did she convey how you would criticize my home. The home in which you were—ever so briefly—a guest and an employee. Tempy, please collect Miss Boudreaux's trunk from the room upstairs. Miss Boudreaux, if your carriage has already departed, we will happily lend you use of ours. Allowing that it's handsome enough for your taste."

The woman stared, slack jawed, and Jake looked between the two women, liking this Mrs. Colonel John McGavock more by the minute. And starting to believe she'd earned that title.

Miss Boudreaux huffed. "I have never been asked to leave a position before!"

"Well, there's always a first time. As I tell my

children when they stumble and fall, learn from the experience. Take the lesson and just enough of the pain to remember not to repeat the same mistake again. I'll see you out now."

The tiny black woman skirted by Jake, a ghost of a smile touching her mouth. And Jake looked over at Mrs. McGavock. "I'll help her with the trunk, ma'am."

"That would be much appreciated, Captain."

Minutes later, Jake stood inside the open front doorway alongside Mrs. McGavock and Tempy as the wheels of *Chef* Boudreaux's carriage struggled for purchase on the ice-slicked drive leading back to town.

He smiled. "And I thought that by coming here I was leaving the front lines behind me."

Mrs. McGavock laughed. "Life is too short and our days too few to willfully spend time in the company of people who insist on telling us how much better they are than everyone else."

"Amen to that," Tempy whispered, which drew more laughter. "Come on back to the kitchen now, Captain Winston, and I'll get you some potato soup that'll warm up your insides real good. And how do you feel about butter cookies?"

Later that night in the cabin, Jake ran a hand over his smooth jawline, his face cool without his beard.

"My, my," Tempy had said when he'd shown up freshly shaven for dinner with the McGavocks. "Miracle what a difference a razor can make in a man."

Remembering the mirth in her eyes, he smiled as he added more wood to the hearth. But he still couldn't get the chimney to draw properly. Marking the chimney as an item to be investigated tomorrow, he settled for what heat it provided and crawled into bed—a clean ticking stuffed with fresh straw—and pulled the blanket up over him. How long had it been since he'd slept in so nice a bed?

For nearly two years now his bedroll and whatever patch of hopefully dry earth he could find had been where he'd laid his head. To have a cabin with a roof over his head and a fire burning in the hearth seemed an extravagance. And felt almost wrong. Especially when he thought of his fellow soldiers encamped in the bitter cold and snow.

The cabin boasted two rooms down and two up, and—all but for this room—was being used as storage. It was clean enough, but he looked forward to getting it into better shape. The front door stuck on one side and needed planing. There were spaces around the windows where the mortar had cracked and fallen away and cold air poured in. He could patch those spots easily enough. And the chimney was already on his list. He'd be here for the better part of a month, after all, much to his dismay. And he'd been taught to leave a place better than he'd found it.

The flame in the oil lamp flickered on a tiny side table and cast undulating shadows on the walls, the darkness playing hide-and-seek with the light. He wondered about the slaves who'd lived in this cabin through the years. Mrs. McGavock had said they'd been sent south. And depending on who won this war, they might or might not be back.

But he wasn't fighting this war to keep Negroes enslaved. If he had his druthers, he'd free the lot of them. A free man worked harder and contributed more to society than a slave ever did. And he'd known enough Negroes throughout his life to know that they weren't so different from white men. There were good men and bad, be they dark skinned or light. It was what lay within a man that really counted.

At supper tonight he'd met Colonel McGavock and found the man to be formidable. Rather a suitable match for Colonel Carrie, as he'd taken to thinking of Mrs. McGavock upon learning her first name this evening. Had a good ring to it, he thought, even if he'd never dare use the name aloud. He'd met the couple's children too. A girl, Hattie, around eight, he thought. Then the young boy, Winder, whom he'd already seen running with Andrew.

As he leaned to turn down the lamp, an image from earlier that day returned and Jake reached for his notebook and pencil instead. He sat up, shoved the pillow behind his back, and turned to a fresh page, choosing to ignore the familiar twinge in his left shoulder. This notebook was almost full. He needed to get another one from town soon.

He closed his eyes for a moment, the image of Andrew looking up at his mother returning with clarity. The adoration in the boy's eyes, the confusion warring with the desire—the need—to trust and believe that his mother really did know best.

The curves and planes of the boy's face took shape on the page as Jake paused frequently, patient for the image to resurface in his memory, and to sharpen. He rubbed his eyes, then reached into his knapsack on the floor for his eyeglasses and slipped them on. Just like that, the lines cleared.

No sooner did he finish that drawing than another came to him, and he turned the page. But he found her face less clear to him. Yet her eyes, he remembered her eyes and drew them as she'd looked peering up at him, a sadness lingering beneath her expression even as she'd smiled. And her smile, he remembered that too.

He began drawing her lips, the way they curved and—

Then it hit him. What he was doing. He lifted his pencil from the page. Mrs. *Warren* Prescott. He stared into her eyes for a moment, then closed the notebook and blew out the lamp.

The glow from the fire bathed the room in orangey red, and as the minutes ticked silently past, that same unwanted tug of reminiscence he'd felt earlier returned.

He was twenty-eight. Had never been married, never had children. And had all but accepted, at least earlier on, that he'd likely die in this war. So somewhere along the way he'd convinced himself it was best that he didn't have anyone waiting back home for him. Best that he no longer even had a home.

But as weeks had turned into months, and as he'd made it through battles unscathed—until recently—he'd begun to think that maybe he would live through it after all. Not that he was invincible, as Colonel Stratton had said, and as his current condition confirmed. But that perhaps, one day, he might have what his parents had had.

But there was something dangerous about embracing that kind of hope. About giving part of your heart to someone else. He'd seen evidence of that again today. In her. And in Andrew. He could only imagine how much Warren Prescott missed his family, loved and cared for them, was eager to be reunited with them.

Jake stared into the flames, sleep a far piece away, and he found himself praying for a man he'd never met, all for the sake of a woman and child he scarcely knew.

CHAPTER 8

"I-I'm sorry. I don't understand." Seated opposite Mrs. McGavock in the family parlor, Aletta searched her expression, unable to believe what she was hearing. She'd held off returning to Carnton over the weekend, scarcely able to wait until Monday morning came. "I thought you already had a pastry chef who—"

"Yes, I did, Mrs. Prescott. However, circumstances changed quite suddenly on Friday afternoon after your departure. And since you said you would return this morning to discuss the details of the nativity you're to build, I decided to wait and offer you the position, rather certain you would still be interested. I hope I am correct in my assumption."

"Yes, ma'am, you are. Of course." Aletta's mind raced.

"Very good then. We're in need of someone gifted at making pastries and sweets, pies and cookies and such. And based upon what you said during your visit last week—that you worked in a bakery at one time and that your mother, once a head cook, instructed you—I trust you still possess those skills you learned."

It wasn't a question. "Yes, Mrs. McGavock. Although I can't guarantee that my creations will be as fancy as a master chef's."

"The Lord Jesus is not impressed with outward show, and neither am I, Mrs. Prescott. Simple but delicious is what will please me. Can you do that?"

"Absolutely, I can. Yes, ma'am."

"Very well then. You're hired. For a second time," Mrs. McGavock added, eyebrow arching. "First as our nativity scene maker, however much that may concern me." She gave Aletta a look. "And second, as cook and pastry chef. You'll be paid accordingly for both positions. Unless you wish to change your mind about crafting the booth and manger. You may find it to be too taxing with the other responsibilities."

"Oh no. With Captain Winston's help, I'll manage very well, I'm sure. Besides, I've already told Andrew about the life-size nativity scene, and he's looking forward to his turn as Joseph. Either that or dressing up as an attending cow or sheep."

They both laughed, and Aletta sat a little straighter.

Her back ached from the long walk from town. How she would manage to accomplish everything, she didn't know. But she wasn't about to turn down paying positions. Especially not positions she knew she was qualified for. Granted, the tasks would've been more easily undertaken if she wasn't seven months pregnant.

She'd returned home last Friday to find a formal notice of foreclosure proceedings from the bank along with a declaration stating that she and Andrew were to vacate the home no later than the third of December. She'd worried about it all weekend, had gotten little sleep. And yet, looking back on it now, she could see that God had been working on her behalf, even though she'd been blind to it. He was providing the money for her to find another place for them to live.

Her faith felt so small in comparison to his loving kindness.

Mrs. McGavock refilled both of their teacups. "You've already met Tempy, who has expressed her pleasure at my offering you the position. So I trust the two of you will be able to share the kitchen amiably."

"Oh, quite, Mrs. McGavock. And it's such a fine kitchen too. So spacious and with the large hearth. You and your husband planned well."

"Actually it was my late in-laws, Mr. and Mrs. Randal McGavock, God rest them both, who planned well. They married in 1811, then built a home on the property some fifteen years later. The wing of the house where the kitchen is located is that home. The main house we're in now is what they built some eleven years later. The wing of the house is where my husband lived in his younger years. So it holds special meaning to us both. And I hope it will to you as well, as soon as I explain the other condition of the job."

Aletta didn't quite follow.

"The pastry chef the committee originally hired was to start this past Friday, and our agreement with her—based on the responsibilities of the position—included room and board. Because even though the auction doesn't formally begin until the seventeenth of December, we have much preparation to do between now and then. Not to mention the Thanksgiving celebration this week. Which means that you'll need to reside here at Carnton beginning today, if possible, Mrs. Prescott. Only temporarily, of course, until we get through Christmas and possibly the New Year."

Aletta blinked. "Live here. At Carnton."

"Yes, that's right. And I believe it will work out nicely. I've spoken with Miss Clouston, our nanny and the children's tutor, and she's willing to instruct Andrew as well. Miss Clouston believes that having your son in the classroom might actually help my dear Winder to pay closer attention. We'll have to wait and see if her theory proves correct. But I trust it will. Miss Clouston hasn't failed us yet." Mrs. McGavock gestured toward the window. "See for yourself at how well our sons are getting along."

Aletta turned to see the boys running and chasing each other outside, a November sun shining brightly as the boys' breath puffed white in the cold. She could scarcely take it all in. She had a job, albeit temporarily. But far more than that, she and Andrew had a safe place to live—with a friend for him, and schooling—through the first of the year. And perhaps, if she worked hard and proved her worth, beyond that.

Although she didn't dare set her hopes so high.

"Which brings me back to that wing of the house, Mrs. Prescott. There are three bedrooms above the kitchen. Tempy and Miss Clouston each reside in one, and you and your son will take the third bedroom on the very end. Nearest to the smokehouse, I'm afraid, which is about to become quite potent with the aroma of smoked bacon and ham once the hog killing is under way. *If* this entire situation is agreeable to you, of course."

"It's most agreeable, Mrs. McGavock." Aletta worked to keep the emotion from her voice. "Thank you, ma'am, for your trust in me."

Mrs. McGavock eyed her. "I do trust you, Mrs. Prescott, and I'm grateful for your willingness to help with the auction with such enthusiasm. It's a cause that's so important. Both to the soldiers and to the community." She paused. "I admire you, Mrs. Prescott. I don't know what I'd do if I were in your situation. I only hope I would handle it half as well."

Aletta shook her head. "I do my best, ma'am. Especially for Andrew's sake. But there are moments when despair is an unwelcome but very near companion."

"I've no doubt of that, Mrs. Prescott. And yet . . . here you are."

Aletta smiled, then listened with interest as Mrs. McGavock laid out the plans for the auction including the work leading up to it. So much to do—sewing, knitting, cooking, quilting. So much organization. But it excited her to be a part of something that would help so many, and that would keep her mind occupied and her hands busy.

Finally, Mrs. McGavock rose, and Aletta took that as her cue.

"I believe that's all the information I have for you at present, Mrs. Prescott. I'm going to the kitchen to discuss this week's menus with Tempy. I'll ask her to fetch Captain Winston for you. He can take you into town for your personal items and whatever else you might require. No need for you to walk all that way again in the cold."

"Thank you, Mrs. McGavock." Aletta looked again at the large portrait of her hostess situated on the far wall. The mistress of Carnton in more youthful years.

Mrs. McGavock laughed softly. "That was painted shortly before my marriage to Mr. McGavock. Some fifteen years ago. And another lifetime, it feels like."

"It's beautiful, ma'am." Yet Aletta found it somewhat odd that Mrs. McGavock had chosen to wear what appeared to be black for the portrait, the color of death, at what had to have been so joyous a time in her life. Although, on closer look, perhaps the color of the dress was a deep midnight blue instead. Regardless, the portrait, and the woman in it, were lovely.

"Why don't you wait here, Mrs. Prescott, until Captain Winston has pulled the wagon around. And Miss Clouston will make certain Andrew is taken care of until you've returned."

"Thank you, ma'am."

Mrs. McGavock took her leave, and Aletta walked toward a rear-facing window of the home when her gaze fell to a newspaper folded in half on a side table. She looked more closely. Today's date. And the newspaper had already been well read. Assuming she had a few moments, she picked it up and scanned the headlines, looking for updates on the war, any news that might indicate a near end to the conflict.

She came upon an update from the War Department. And more from habit than anything else, she scanned the three lists for Tennessee— "Killed, Wounded, and Missing"—hoping she wouldn't recognize any of the names.

Nearing the end of the first list, she read the last name and it delivered an unexpected blow.

Emmett Zachary, Franklin, TN

Her eyes filled. No . . . Her hand went to her chest. Not Emmett, Warren's friend. Kate's husband. She closed her eyes as tears rose. She'd only met Emmett once. Briefly, at the train station. But Warren had spoken of him so often in his letters. They'd become good friends.

Aletta swallowed, resolved to go by and visit Kate while in town that afternoon, offer her condolences and see if there was anything she could do for her. Kate had done so much for her earlier that fall. Had been such a comfort.

Aletta returned the newspaper to the table and went to peer out the back window and across the large back porch. She rubbed the ache in the small of her back, the pain gradually beginning to subside.

She spotted Captain Winston in the barn, hitching the mares to the wagon, and walked out to join him. When he turned around, she was taken aback.

"Good morning, Mrs. Prescott."

She stared at the freshly shaven man smiling down at her, a hint of stubble shadowing the jawline that only yesterday had sported a full and unruly beard. "Captain Winston?"

His smile deepened, along with the gray of his eyes, which, without the distraction of the beard, proved to be a rather disarming combination.

He rubbed a hand over his jaw as though privy to her thoughts. "Yes, ma'am. At your service. Mrs. McGavock says you need to go into town."

"Y-yes, I do. Thank you, Captain, for taking me."

"My pleasure. Just give me a couple more minutes and we'll be set." He circled the wagon and checked the harness straps on the other side.

She tried not to stare, but had to acknowledge . . . He was a handsome man with strong, angular features. And younger than she would've guessed upon their first meeting. He possessed a quiet confidence about him as though he had nothing left to prove. Either that, or he simply didn't put much stock in others' opinions.

Seeing him clean shaven brought back memories of Warren's last trip home in April. He'd been sporting a similar soldier's beard, as she'd called it. All wild and woolly. She'd shaved it off for him that first night, cherishing the chance to look fully into the face of the man she'd married. And loved. Loved still.

"Allow me, ma'am."

Aletta became aware of Captain Winston's outstretched hand and accepted his assistance

114

up to the bench seat. He settled in beside her.

"Mrs. McGavock tells me you need to go by your house to fetch a few items."

"Yes, that's right. And also—" The mere thought of Kate Zachary and the pain she must be experiencing at that moment, if the woman even knew about Emmett's fate yet, caused a tightening in her chest. "I need to go see a friend. I read the War Department's list moments earlier and . . . learned that her husband has been killed."

He looked over. "I'm sorry to hear that."

She nodded, emotion rising to her eyes. "Kate was there for me when I got the news about Warren," she whispered. "And I want to be there for her."

He stilled. "Your husband . . . was killed?"

She bowed her head. "Yes . . . Only last month."

He said nothing for a moment, then a deep sigh left him. "I-I didn't know, Mrs. Prescott. I'm . . . I'm so very sorry."

A moment passed before she could finally look over at him, and the empathy in his expression was nearly her undoing. "Thank you, Captain Winston," she whispered.

He held her gaze for what felt like a long time but was probably only a handful of heartbeats. Then he turned, gathered the reins, and started for town.

• • •

Jake kept his gaze on the road, resisting the urge to sneak a look at Mrs. Prescott seated beside him on the bench seat. Her husband was dead. She was with child, already had a small boy, and her husband wasn't coming home. Mrs. McGavock hadn't said anything about that to him. Then again, why would she? She'd told him about hiring Mrs. Prescott as the new pastry chef, which included room and board, and that was about it.

They rode in silence, Mrs. Prescott's hands knotted in her lap, and he wondered exactly how far along with child she was, not that he was about to ask.

He recalled Miss Boudreaux's less than graceful exit on Friday and silently congratulated Colonel Carrie on her decision to hire the better woman. He could easily imagine Mrs. Prescott cooking and baking in the kitchen alongside Tempy. And imagined that Tempy would welcome her presence.

Moments passed, and the low coo of a mourning dove drew his attention. He casually looked off toward the side of the road and searched the thicket of pines, but the icy branches were only a frustrating blur. Seconds later, the call sounded again, as he'd suspected it would, and he faced forward. He gave a slow nod, just once, aware of Mrs. Prescott seemingly lost in thought beside him. And he found it reassuring to know Confederate brothers were close at hand.

When they reached the edge of town, she turned to him.

"It's not far. Two streets up on the right," she said softly. Then a moment later, she pointed. "There. That's the Zacharys' house. The one with the yellow shutters."

Jake brought the wagon to a stop and set the brake. He climbed down and assisted her down as well. "I'll wait here for you."

"If you have an errand to see to, Captain, I could meet you in town somewhere. I'm fine to walk."

"I'll wait here for you, ma'am," he repeated softly, and noticed her eyes begin to fill with tears.

She nodded and walked to the door. She bowed her head, and a moment passed before she knocked. When the door finally opened, a woman appeared and the two of them simply stared at each other for several seconds. Jake began to wonder whether Mrs. Zachary had even received the news. Then he saw the newspaper clutched in her grip and heard a strangled cry as she threw her arms around Mrs. Prescott.

He looked away, the moment demanding privacy. And when he looked back the stoop was empty, the door closed.

He climbed back into the wagon and settled

in to wait, senses alert, grateful for the sunshine despite the cold. He pulled his rifle sight from his pocket, the one his father had given him years ago, and carefully wiped the lens. For as long as he could remember, he'd had the ability to shoot. And not just to shoot, but to shoot well. Better than anyone else around him. And to think that he might have lost that ability made him feel so much less a soldier. So much less a man.

He lifted the scope to his eyes and peered through it as he'd done thousands of times. He adjusted the lens. And again. Then sighed. Would his world ever be clear again? He'd spent some time over the weekend applying the poultices and compresses the doctor had prescribed. But same as before, he couldn't tell a lick of difference.

And yet, knowing what he knew now about Mrs. Prescott and her son, Andrew, gave his own situation fresh perspective. Still, he prayed his change in sight was only temporary and that by the time he left here, it would be restored.

He'd crawled up onto the roof of the cabin on Saturday and quickly discovered why the chimney wouldn't draw. With some mortar from Colonel McGavock, he'd repaired the crumbled brick and cleaned out the flue. After sealing the cracks in the mortar around the windows and planing and rehanging the door, the cabin now stayed nice and toasty. And he'd enjoyed the work. Felt good to take something and make it better.

A sound brought him around and Jake looked back toward the house.

Mrs. Prescott stepped out, whispered something to the woman in the doorway, then drew her into a hug. Eyes closed, Mrs. Zachary nodded.

Jake assisted Mrs. Prescott into the wagon then climbed up beside her.

"She's going to be all right," she said softly, her tone more hopeful than confident, almost as though she were attempting to convince herself that she was going to be all right too.

She sniffed and dabbed at the corners of her eyes, and Jake found himself praying for her yet again. Only this time, for her and Andrew alone.

"Kate said that her husband, Emmett"—her voice was barely audible—"was killed in battle two weeks ago. Yet his body had been so badly wounded . . ." She looked away. "The War Department said they couldn't identify him at first. Finally, they managed to piece together a letter found in his pocket and that's how—" She firmed her jaw, her breath coming hard now. "I *hate* this war," she said through clenched teeth, tears slipping down her cheeks.

"I know," he whispered. "I do too."

She pulled a handkerchief from her sleeve. "Emmett and my husband met each other in camp and became friends. They fought alongside each other. Warren often said that Emmett was the brother he'd never had. They even favored each other." She gave a little smile, and in that simple, beautiful act, Jake glimpsed a measure of her strength.

He looked down at his hands. How many men had he watched die since this war had started? How many had he killed? How many women out there were grieving much like this one beside him, and Mrs. Zachary, because their husbands or fathers or sons or brothers weren't coming home? It wasn't a question new to him.

Yet in that moment, it had an edge to it that cut deeper than it had before. He released the brake and snapped the reins.

She gave him directions to the Presbyterian church, and he headed that way.

"I want to stop by and see the facility. That's where we'll host the gatherings before the auction."

"Gatherings *before* the auction?"

"Yes, where the women will meet to knit gloves, scarves, socks, and caps for the soldiers, and to write letters of encouragement. The children will draw pictures for the soldiers too. We'll also form several quilting circles, then we'll auction off the quilts. Closer to the actual date of the event, the other hired cooks will come to Carnton and we'll bake and cook for all the attendees. Mrs. McGavock says they're expecting hundreds of people to come from Nashville and the surrounding communities."

Hearing the tender pride in her voice, Jake nodded. "Yes, Mrs. McGavock told me."

The church was unlocked and they let themselves inside. No sign of the preacher as they looked around, Mrs. Prescott peering inside rooms and commenting on occasion.

"We can set up some tables over there." She pointed. "And the ladies can visit as they knit. We'll need patterns, but Mrs. McGavock says she and the other ladies have plenty of those. Oh! And we'll need to buy skeins of yarn too. Mrs. McGavock told me she has enough to get us started. But eventually we'll need to purchase more."

Jake just nodded. He wasn't about to say anything to discourage her, but again he considered how much easier it would be—and maybe even more profitable—if the women would simply donate the funds, let the army buy what they needed, and be done with it.

"What?" she asked softly.

He shook his head. "I didn't say anything."

"I know. But you were thinking something."

He looked into those soft blue eyes and realized he was going to have to hold his cards a little closer to his vest. He smiled and gestured toward the hallway. "After you."

She sighed and walked back outside. "Before

121

we go by my house, I need to stop by the lumber-yard and get the supplies for the nativity."

He paused. "The lumberyard? I bet Colonel McGavock has enough spare pieces around the barn that you could use."

She accepted his help up to the bench seat. "Mrs. McGavock was explicit in her instructions. She said to go to the lumberyard and that a Mr. Harban would supply whatever I needed."

He held up a hand as he claimed the space beside her. "Then to the lumberyard we go. But I know for certain there are a couple of pieces of wood in the barn back at Carnton. Enough for a child's nativity."

"A child's nativity? I'm not making a child's nativity, Captain Winston. I'm building a life-sized booth and manger that will stand in the front yard by the house at Carnton. The children will all take turns playing Mary and Joseph and the shepherds over the course of the auction."

He stared. "You're making a *real* nativity?"

She nodded.

"*You* are?"

He smiled. She didn't.

"My father was a master carpenter, Captain Winston, and he taught me a thing or two about woodworking."

Jake tried to curb his grin but couldn't. The image of her with a hammer and saw sparked amusement. "But you're—" He gestured.

"A woman?"

"Well . . . yes, ma'am. You're obviously a woman. But you're also . . ." He stared, not wanting to say it. And definitely making certain he didn't look down.

"With child," she finally supplied, an eyebrow rising.

"Yes, ma'am. With child."

"Which precludes me from being able to build something?"

He laughed softly. "Which makes a project that would already be a challenge even more so."

Her eyes narrowed the slightest bit. "For one, it won't be a challenge. I'll only need your help toward the end, when it comes to nailing the larger pieces together. And secondly, I've already drawn out the plans. I have all the measurements and the list of required supplies." She pulled a piece of paper from her reticule and handed it to him.

He unfolded it, and his smile faded. He looked over at her. "You're serious."

This time she was the one to laugh, though the action held no humor. "Yes, Captain. I'm serious. Now, please, I need to go to the lumberyard, then stop by my house for some of my and Andrew's things, then return to Carnton so I can begin baking."

"Baking? But the auction isn't for another two weeks."

She lifted her chin slightly. "Mrs. McGavock not only hired me to bake for the auction, but also wants me to help with the Thanksgiving celebration this week. And to cook and prepare meals for the volunteers who'll begin meeting the last day of November. Only a week from today."

He nodded. Cooking and baking he could see her doing. But building a nativity like the one shown in the plans? With a roof and sides and a manger to boot? And her being with child? It felt like he was peering at the world through his rifle sight again.

When they reached the lumberyard, Mrs. Prescott climbed down from the wagon without his assistance. A show of independence, no doubt. Jake opened the door to the building for her, and she preceded him inside. But the owner still addressed him first.

"Yes, sir. What can I do for you today?"

"You're Mr. Harban?" Mrs. Prescott said, taking the lead. At the man's nod, she stepped forward and introduced herself. "Mrs. McGavock from Carnton instructed me to ask for you."

Jake hung back, watching the scene, and knew what his own expression must have looked like a while earlier when Mrs. Prescott had pulled the diagram of the nativity from her reticule and handed it to him. Because Mr. Harban wore the same perplexed look now as he walked away, marching orders in hand.

"Captain Winston, would you please drive the wagon around to the side of the building so they can load up the supplies?"

He gave a quick salute. "Yes, ma'am, General Prescott."

Glimpsing a hint of humor in her eyes, he did as she asked, and soon they were on their way to her house, wagon bed loaded with what would be the finest nativity Franklin, Tennessee, had ever seen. *If* the finished product ended up looking anything like the drawing she'd shown him, a feat that was still highly questionable in his mind.

CHAPTER 9

She'd have to be blind to miss the man's disapproval. Not only about her building the nativity, but also, it seemed, about the auction in general. Aletta stole a furtive glance at Captain Winston seated on the bench beside her, trying to read him. And failing.

But his silence as she'd shared the plans for the activities prior to and during the auction had been deafening. Which she found puzzling. Because the Women's Relief Society was doing all of this to help the wounded soldiers, of which he was one—despite how *un*wounded the man appeared to be.

So why wouldn't he be in favor of it? And why exactly was he listed as being wounded?

She'd seen him carrying crates and boxes, hitching the team to the wagon. And even now he'd helped load the supplies back at the lumberyard. Precisely why wasn't he back with his regiment fighting with the others? Unless . . . he'd seized the opportunity and had volunteered to come to Carnton in order to escape battle.

"Turn up ahead. On Vine. It's the second house on the left."

She'd heard of deserters, men who fled north to escape the war, and even of soldiers who abandoned their posts in the middle of the night and simply walked away. After some of the stories Warren had told her, she could see how that would be a—

The house came into view and every thought fell away as a loneliness, deep and insatiable, moved over her, along with a yearning for Warren and the life they'd shared. How was she going to raise not one child, but two, without their father? After Christmas had passed and her duties at Carnton were no longer required, what then? Where would she go? Who would be with her when it came time for the baby to be born?

A strand of fear wove itself around her heart and pulled tight, and she found it difficult to breathe.

Captain Winston brought the wagon to a stop by the walkway, then looked over at her. "Are you all right?" he asked softly.

She nodded, not speaking until she was certain her voice would hold. "It should only take me a few minutes to pack the trunks."

"Signal when you're done. I'll come inside and get them." He set the brake and quickly climbed down, then assisted her.

Packing took even less time than she'd estimated, and she realized how many items she'd either sold or bartered in recent months in exchange for necessities. She'd have to come back soon for what little furniture and whatnot remained—and for Warren's clothes. She had no idea where she'd store the items, but she'd worry about that later. She only knew she wasn't ready to part with his personal items yet. It was too soon.

Trunks packed, she opened the front door and waved, and Captain Winston strode toward her. She watched for a limp or even the slightest hiccup in his gait. But whatever injury he'd sustained didn't affect his manner of walking.

She didn't know why, because she didn't know him well by any means, but it bothered her to think that he was the type of man who would try to cheat his way out of doing his duty. Because she wouldn't have thought that about him based upon first impression.

She stepped aside for him to enter the home, but he hesitated.

"It might be better, Mrs. Prescott, if you stay out here on the porch while I go in. Just tell me which room the trunks are in, and I'll retrieve them."

Hearing what he wasn't saying, she stepped out onto the porch. "Yes, of course, Captain. You're right." She told him where to find the trunks, and he went inside.

As she waited, she thought of the afternoon she'd arrived early to MaryNell's and discovered MaryNell's *friend* there. Aletta looked across the street, then down both ways. No one in sight, but she still felt better leaving no room for even a hint of impropriety.

As Captain Winston loaded the trunks into the back of the wagon, she locked the front door then accepted his assistance up to the bench seat. It occurred to her then that she didn't even know if the Captain was married. He wore no wedding ring. But that meant little these days, as she knew. Yet he hadn't mentioned anything about having a wife or family.

He snapped the reins and the team responded.

As they rode in silence, she debated within herself about whether he was a man of character—as his behavior back at the house would lead her to believe—or perhaps a shirker. Finally, as he guided the wagon up the drive leading to Carnton and the house came into view, she could take no more.

"I understand from Mrs. McGavock that you were recently wounded, Captain Winston."

He said nothing for a moment, then looked over at her. "That's right."

She waited for more of an explanation, but none came. And the silence stretched. She couldn't account for the frustrating sense of wanting more of an answer. She only knew she couldn't let it go.

"And . . . how were you wounded?"

He kept his focus ahead. "I was shot, Mrs. Prescott. In the shoulder."

Aletta felt the air slowly seep from her lungs. Something about the way he said it, or maybe the way he didn't look over at her, made her feel as if he questioned her motive in asking. Which, given what she'd been thinking, he would've had a right to do, had he been privy to the fact.

"I'm sorry, Captain. I . . . imagine that was very difficult."

He eyed her briefly. "It hurt a mite."

Feeling more than a little put in her place, she kept her focus on the road. But as she thought again about how "loud" his silence had been back at the church, she soon found the same pesky sense of frustration returning.

"Captain, do you not believe the auction to be a worthy pursuit?"

He smiled then. But still didn't look at her. "What I think, Mrs. Prescott, is that my opinion doesn't matter in this regard."

"So you *don't* believe it's a worthy pursuit."

"I didn't say that, ma'am." He glanced away, and took his time before responding again. "I think the auction is a well-intentioned event."

"A *well-intentioned* event?"

"Yes, ma'am. I think all that you and Mrs. McGavock and the other ladies have planned is very nice. And very generous. And I hope it raises a lot of money for the cause. Because the soldiers, we sure need it." He paused. "It just seems like an awful lot of work to get there."

She turned on the bench seat. "A lot of work that won't amount to much good? That's what you're saying?"

"No, ma'am. I did not say that. I believe it'll amount to a lot of good. I simply think that some-times"—his grip tightened on the reins and the levity left his expression—"there's a faster way to get something done, that's all." He brought the wagon to a stop in front of the house. "I don't say that to upset you, Mrs. Prescott. And I never would've volunteered my opinion had you not inquired."

"Well . . . I suppose that will teach me *not* to inquire."

He climbed down and was on his way around to help her, but she quickly managed it on her own again, feeling a small—if not a tad silly—sense of accomplishment. "You're right. There are faster ways to get things done."

He just stared.

"Thank you for your help today, Captain Winston. Now would you please unload the supplies for the nativity into the barn? I need to go inside and check on Andrew, then begin helping with dinner. Good day."

She didn't wait for a response but strode toward the house, yet his quiet voice still reached her.

"You're most welcome . . . General Prescott."

Not daring to look back, she couldn't keep from smiling.

Two nights later, after helping Tempy with Thanksgiving meal preparations for the following day, Aletta grabbed her shawl and slipped out to the barn, oil lamp in one hand, nativity design in the other.

Tired though she was, she was eager to at least get the measurements drawn onto the pieces of wood so she'd be ready to begin cutting come the weekend. And with Andrew situated before the hearth, tucked between Winder and Hattie as Miss Clouston read them a bedtime story, now was her chance to get the measuring done quickly. Without her precious son's "assistance."

"Measure twice, cut once," she spoke aloud into the quiet, recalling her father's treasured counsel. She'd get all the pieces of wood measured and marked tonight, then would check the measurements against the plans once again on Saturday before cutting.

Captain Winston had stacked all the boards atop one another on one side of the barn, placing the largest boards on the bottom. But no bother.

If she could chop firewood, she could certainly move a few pieces of wood.

She hung the oil lamp on a peg and laid aside her design and shawl. First, to get the largest pieces laid flat where she could assess everything and get clean measurements, and make certain she wasn't forgetting anything. She moved the bags of nails atop the pile, then started to lift the first piece of wood—

But it proved heavier than she'd wagered. Even the smallest pieces were heavy. Stubbornness demanded she try again. But sensibility and awareness of her body's limits, especially being with child, swiftly won out.

She sighed, hands on hips.

Knowing what she needed to do, she still considered asking Tempy for help first. But Tempy, though strong, would be no better equipped to lift these pieces of wood than she was. Nor should a woman Tempy's age be enlisted to do such a thing.

Aletta glanced in the general direction of Captain Winston's cabin. He would help her, she had no doubt. But at what cost to her womanly pride? If only she hadn't made such a point of telling him she wouldn't require his assistance until the final stages of the project. She blew out a breath.

And here she was, not even started yet, and already she needed him.

. . .

A knock sounded and Jake paused in his sketching. Pencil and notebook in hand, he rose from the rocking chair by the fire and opened the door.

"Mrs. Prescott?" He glanced beyond her toward the main house, the cold forcing its way inside. "Is everything all right?"

"Yes, everything's fine." She tugged her shawl closer about her shoulders. "I . . . have a favor to ask of you, that's all." Her gaze fell to the notebook in his hand. "*If* I'm not bothering you."

He glanced down to see his partially finished sketch of the McGavocks' pecan grove. "No, you're not bothering me." He hesitated, then gestured. "Would you like to step inside? It's freezing out."

Uncertainty shadowed her expression. Whether about his invitation or her reason for being here, he didn't know. But she finally shook her head. "I need you to help me, if you would. With the nativity," she added quickly.

And Jake suddenly realized it wasn't uncertainty in her expression he saw. It was irritation. And he curbed a smile, knowing only too well— even just having met her—how much it likely rankled her to have to come here and ask for his help.

But how very glad he was that she had.

He laid aside the pencil and sketch pad, grabbed

134

his coat, and draped it around her shoulders. "Lead the way, ma'am."

They hurried into the barn, and he closed the door behind them. He wasn't about to say "I told you so." But it was obvious she'd realized she needed help building the nativity after all. Which was understandable. And he was only too glad to step in.

"Thank you, Captain Winston. Both for your coat and for your help."

He accepted the jacket and laid it aside, choosing not to make her grovel. "I've been thinking a lot about how best to design the booth for the nativity, Mrs. Prescott, and it seems to me that . . ."

As he detailed his plan, perplexity shaded her features.

Finally, he paused. "Am I going too fast?"

She stared. "Not at all. But I didn't ask you here to help me with the design. I already know what I want to do. I simply need you to move the wood so I can make some measurements. It's too heavy for me to lift."

He looked at the pile of wood, then back at her. "So . . . you don't need my ideas."

She smiled and shook her head, a glint in her eyes. "Only your brawn, Captain Winston."

Enjoying the smart little quirk in her tone, he felt only mildly insulted as he spent the next hour and a half moving the stack of wood, waiting while she measured it and consulted with her original plans, then moving it all back again, out of the way of foot traffic. All while conversation—and comfortable spaces of silence—settled easily between them.

"So you've lived here in Franklin all your life?" he asked as he moved the final board, measured and marked, back onto the stack.

She nodded.

"No siblings?"

"I was the only child born to my parents. What about you? Any brothers or sisters?"

Jake paused, fingering a callus on his palm. "I had a younger brother, Freddie. But . . . he died at Vicksburg."

She stared at him, her gaze glistening in the glow of the oil lamp. "I'm so sorry, Captain Winston. My husband, Warren, wrote to me about what happened there. In far greater detail than I'd read about in the newspapers." She briefly closed her eyes, her brow furrowing. "The images his letters conjured haunt me even now. I cannot fathom how . . ."

Her voice faded and a barrage of all too painful memories rushed in to fill the silence. For them both, Jake wagered by her expression. With no small effort, he concentrated on recalling Freddie's smile, the way his brother used to laugh and poke fun every chance he got.

"I wish," she whispered, her voice unsteady, "I

wish I knew how my husband died." Slowly, she lifted her gaze. "All the letter said was that he'd been killed in battle, and that the army would inform me of the details as they learned them. *If* they learned them."

Jake studied her features in the flame's amber glow, wishing he could offer her more hope. But he'd walked the aftermath of war, and knew better.

She turned and began gathering the tools she'd used into a worn leather pouch. "I've forgotten how much closer I feel to my father when I have a hand plane or chisel in my grip."

"Those were his," Jake said softly.

She nodded. "Except for the mallet. Andrew and I gave that to Warren for Christmas three years ago." Reminiscence softened her smile as she fingered the mallet's red handle. "I'd told Andrew we were shopping for Papa, and when Andrew saw the mallet in the mercantile that day, he was convinced this was what we should get."

"Andrew's a fine boy, Mrs. Prescott. You've done well by him." Jake sought and held her gaze. "You both did, ma'am."

The light in her eyes warmed him where he stood.

"Are . . . you married, Captain Winston?"

The question was so unexpected, Jake had to smile. "No, ma'am. I'm not. And never have been."

She nodded and returned to her task. Once everything was put away, he walked with her back to the house, insisting she keep his coat around her shoulders.

"This is the first time I've seen you out of uniform, Captain."

He glanced down at his shirt and dungarees. "You planning on turning me in?"

She acted as though she were weighing that possibility. "Probably not just yet. I might need your help again sometime soon."

He laughed, then offered a bow. "Well, if you do need my help, ma'am, please know in advance that you will always have it."

She smiled up at him, her precise expression inscrutable in the shadows, and Jake found his gaze drawn to the inviting curve of her lips. His thoughts swiftly took a more intimate turn as his imagination led him down a path he knew was best left untrod. And it didn't help his resolve when she didn't look away. He reached up and fingered a loose curl at her temple and heard her breath quicken. He leaned closer, cupping the side of her face, all but able to taste her kiss and the softness of her lips.

"Captain Winston, I—" She took a hasty step backward, her breath coming hard. "I'd best be getting inside. It's late, after all."

The fullness of the moment and of what he'd been about to do hit him brick hard. "Mrs.

Prescott—" Jake winced. "Please. Forgive me, ma'am. I—"

"There's nothing to forgive, Captain." Her smile was brief and unconvincing. "Good night."

Far more hastily than he would've liked, she slipped in through the kitchen door and closed it behind her. Wishing he could recall the last moment and do it differently, he strode back to his cabin.

It wasn't until later that evening, flipping through his sketchbook, that he realized just how much of his thoughts this woman occupied. Just as she did the pages of his notebook. More than was wise, he knew, given his circumstances. And hers.

CHAPTER 10

"Let's go kill us some hogs!" Winder yelled, waving a make-believe sword in his hand. Andrew quickly joined in and both boys raced like the wind toward the field adjacent to the barn. Early morning fog still blanketed the winter grasses and clung to the evergreens on the hills, giving the estate a somewhat ethereal feel.

"Andrew, slow down!" Aletta called, pulling her shawl closer about her shoulders and waiting for Tempy to join her. "And be careful!"

She was none too sure about attending this event to begin with. A hog killing certainly didn't *feel* like a festive Christmas pastime. Though the estate, at least, looked decidedly festive. Jake had hung nearly two dozen ribbon-swathed evergreen wreaths about the barns and fences, per Mrs. McGavock's request, and the sight of Carnton arrayed so beautifully warmed her.

She yawned, her day having started especially early that morning with helping Tempy prepare breakfast for all the workers lending a hand in the event. They'd carried the food to the barn before sunup, then had let the men serve themselves as they arrived while she and Tempy returned to the kitchen to start on the noonday meal. The amount of food they'd prepared still amazed her, as did the McGavocks' generosity in providing it.

"Andrew," she called again. "Stay close. Don't go too far."

"Oh, don't you worry, Missus Prescott." Tempy came up beside her. "Those boys'll be fine. Every boy I ever knowed loves hog killin' day."

"I know I did when I was younger."

Aletta turned to see Captain Winston walking toward them and felt a blush creeping into her cheeks. He smiled at her and she returned the gesture, same as she would to anyone else, she told herself.

Yet she found it impossible to deny her heightened awareness of the man.

No matter that she'd seen him several times over the last four days since Thanksgiving—and had ridden to and from the McGavocks' church with him and Andrew yesterday morning. All she could think about was when he'd walked her back to the house the other night after helping her move the wood. She'd been so startled when he'd leaned in to kiss her. Which had been surprising enough. But what bothered her even more was that she hadn't turned away. At least, not at first.

Here she was, seven months pregnant with

141

Warren's child, and she'd found herself actually wanting Captain Winston to kiss her. Wanting him to take her in his arms and hold her until she could feel the solid beat of his heart against hers. The blush in her face deepened.

Twice, Captain Winston had made polite attempts to speak with her privately, but she'd managed to avoid it, embarrassed and wishing they could simply go back and recapture the ease of their friendship before that moment. Because, as she had that night, she felt awkward and exposed.

But mostly, she felt unfaithful to Warren's memory. And partly responsible.

Tempy peered up at him. "So you done this before then, Captain?"

"Oh yes, ma'am. Many times. I grew up on a farm in South Carolina." He looked around. "It wasn't near what Carnton is, but it was home. And it was special." His voice gained a touch of melancholy.

"This be Missus Prescott's first time."

"Is that so?"

Aletta nodded. "We had chickens and cows, but no pigs."

"Oh, you ain't lived, Missus Prescott, 'til you tasted fresh sausage fried up straight from the grinder." Tempy briefly closed her eyes. "That and warm tenderloin with all them mashed sweet potatoes, greens, and stewed apples we made this mornin'. And backbone stew's good eatin' too!"

Captain Winston smiled. "Backbone stew is the best. Especially with corn bread slathered in butter."

"Tempy!" a woman called. "We need your help over here."

Aletta turned to see a group of women standing beneath a massive elm tree. And near them, a large tub perched over a blazing fire. What looked to be a rope and pulley system had been looped above it over a high branch, and a team of mules stood hitched nearby. Tempy moved to join them and Aletta swiftly fell into step beside her.

"Oh no, Missus Prescott." Tempy laid a hand on her arm. "You best not be helpin' at this station, ma'am. Not your first time. Wait here, and Missus McGavock will be along soon. She'll give you a task."

Aletta found herself somewhat relieved, not at all convinced she wanted to see *any* part of this event quite so close up. And yet she also wasn't, considering the man standing beside her.

"Precisely how much do you know about hog killing, Mrs. Prescott?" the Captain asked.

"I believe the question should be, Captain Winston, how much do I want to know about it?"

"And your answer would be?"

"As little as possible."

He laughed and she found herself smiling a little, too, sensing an olive branch in his demeanor.

"I remember my first hog killing." He looked down. "My father found me crying behind the barn."

"How old were you?"

His brow furrowed. "Twenty-two, I think."

The seriousness of his tone coaxed a laugh from her. And even without addressing the issue wedged squarely between them, she felt the tension between them lessening.

"I was about four years old," he continued. "Maybe five. I don't remember much more about that day, other than what my father said to me."

She found herself waiting, wanting to hear what he said next.

"He told me that, as a boy, he'd had much the same reaction as I'd had. And that while he didn't cry anymore when it came to the task of the day, he told me it was crucial, before we started anything, that we thank God for those animals' deaths and what they meant to us as a family. It meant we would eat for the winter. That we wouldn't go hungry. Although, after that first hog killing, my parents said I refused to eat pork for weeks."

She smiled at the image in her mind of him as a little boy.

"But eventually"—a touch of humor tipped one side of his mouth—"bacon won out, and I gave in."

She couldn't help but laugh. "Bacon *is* a force to be reckoned with."

"Yes, ma'am, it is. Especially fried up good and crisp."

He held her gaze, and she sensed he was about to broach a more delicate topic when she spotted her saving grace walking in their direction. "If you'll excuse me, Captain, I need to see Mrs. McGavock and ask her where she'd like me to work. I wish you the best with . . . whatever it is you're doing today."

His smile came easily. "You too, ma'am."

Aletta joined Mrs. McGavock and, to her relief, the woman asked her to help with seasoning and bagging the sausage as it came ready. That, she could do. Mrs. McGavock even had a stool brought outside for her. And as the women gathered around the tables, visiting and talking as they worked throughout the morning, Aletta found herself looking forward to this week when volunteers from the auction would begin meeting at the church.

Everyone broke for lunch. The men were served first, then the women and children. But for some reason, Aletta wasn't hungry. Not like she usually was. When the group started back for the afternoon, she joined in. But shortly after, she felt a wave of fatigue and rubbed the ache in her lower back.

Tempy came alongside her. "You go on back to the house and rest for a while. Everyone'll understand. I'll keep a watch out for Andrew for you. So will Miss Clouston. I saw her with the two boys earlier havin' themselves a fine ol' time."

Aletta held back for a second. "Are you sure?"

Tempy nodded.

Hesitating only briefly, Aletta touched her arm, and surprise showed in the older woman's expression. "Thank you, Tempy."

A handful of seconds ticked past.

"You most welcome, ma'am."

Aletta removed her soiled apron and walked back to the house, looking up at the window to her and Andrew's room above the kitchen. How had they gotten here? She knew the answer, in one sense, of course. She'd applied for the job, then one thing had led to another. But . . .

It was more the fact of how swiftly life could change. One minute life was fine. And the next, your world was turned upside down, looking nothing like it had before.

She climbed the stairs to her room and didn't bother taking off her shawl before she pulled back the covers and slipped into bed. She'd scarcely laid her head down before sleep claimed her.

Sometime later, she stirred, aware of a chill in the room and of daylight all but faded from the swath of sky her window afforded. She pushed herself up, still groggy but knowing she needed to return to work and do her share. But when she stood, a sharp pain arced across her belly and she doubled over, gasping for breath.

CHAPTER II

Aletta braced herself on the edge of the bed, hands fisting the covers, her breath coming hard. She gritted her teeth and pressed a hand to her belly, feeling the child within her moving. *It's too soon. Too soon . . .*

She squeezed her eyes tight, concentrating, waiting, praying for the pain to pass.

In the space of what was probably a moment—but felt like much longer—the contraction subsided. Her pulse slowed. Even with the chill in the room, her forehead felt sweaty to the touch. She sat crouched on the edge of the bed and drew air into her lungs—in and out, in and out—until all but certain that whatever it was had passed.

She stood with care, pulled on her coat, and made her way downstairs and outside.

The evening sky was purple gray, the sun giving way to night, yet everyone was still hard at work. Torches flickered brightly at the various stations and along the path to the smokehouse. The aroma of freshly cooked pork and corn bread wafted toward her. Her mouth watered and she realized how hungry she was.

She looked for Andrew but couldn't find him. So she searched through the crowd of neighbors and hired help until she spotted Captain Winston walking toward her—with Andrew cradled in his arms.

Alarm shot through her and she hurried toward them.

"He's fine," the Captain whispered as they drew closer. "He just finally ran out of steam, that's all. That, and he has a full belly. Five pieces of sausage, at least. And tenderloin and corn bread. This boy can eat."

Smiling, Aletta brushed back the hair from her son's face and kissed him. He didn't stir. "Thank you, Captain," she said softly.

"Are you feeling better? Tempy said you'd gone to lie down."

"I am. It was good to rest. Although I feel guilty for having napped while the rest of you were out here working."

"The rest of us don't have your reason for being tired, Mrs. Prescott. Besides, I saw you up fixing breakfast long before the day even started."

She looked at him. "You saw me? Did you come by the kitchen and I missed you?"

He opened his mouth as though to respond, then smiled. "Actually, no"—he glanced away—"I-I can see into the kitchen from the front window of my cabin. And when I woke up and looked out, I saw the light in the window, then spotted you standing there. I saw Tempy too, of course," he added quickly. "Not only you."

His expression looked a little like that of a boy caught with his hand in the cookie jar, and the discovery put her at ease, for some reason.

"Are you hungry?" He motioned to a table off to the side. "Roasted pork, fresh sausage, butter beans, and corn bread are ready to eat."

"I think I will, if you don't mind holding him for a moment longer?"

"Not at all. I've enjoyed his company today."

Aletta hurriedly filled a plate that Tempy covered with a cloth.

"Oh wait, ma'am!" Tempy held up a hand. "You gotta have some of Missus McGavock's chow-chow. I make it from an old family recipe. Just opened a fresh jar a while ago." She spooned some onto the plate. "There you go. Now you enjoy!"

Aletta thanked her then joined the Captain again. She held out an arm to take Andrew, accustomed to balancing him on her hip. But the Captain shook his head.

"Let me carry him back to the house for you. We're about done for the day out here anyway. And . . . there's something I'd like to discuss with you."

They retraced her steps to the right wing of the house, Aletta readying herself for a conversation she wasn't eager to have.

"I wrote to my commanding officer two days ago, Mrs. Prescott. I asked him if there was anything he could do to . . . help find out how your husband died. I know it won't bring your husband back, of course. But I also know how painful the not knowing can be."

It took Aletta a moment to find her voice, his admission not what she'd been expecting. "*Thank you,* Captain Winston. That's so kind of you. Truly."

He passed Andrew to her, their bodies touching in the transfer, and she met the Captain's gaze—and felt that unexpected stirring inside her again. She became intensely aware of him—his broad shoulders, the kindness in his eyes, in his character, the strong line of his jaw, the way that same lock of hair always fell across his forehead. Hearing the disturbing tone of her thoughts, she quickly looked away.

"Do you have him?" he asked softly, seemingly unaffected.

"Yes. Thank you." But even as she said it, her plate slipped from her grip, and was saved only by Captain Winston's swift reflexes.

"Whoa there," he said, laughing. "Tell you what . . . Why don't I carry this inside for you? Put it on a table in the kitchen."

She balanced Andrew on one hip as the boy tucked his face into the crook of her neck, his soft breath warm on her skin. Captain Winston opened the kitchen door for them, and Aletta stepped inside, her thoughts and emotions swirling. She turned up the oil lamp left burning low on the stove top.

"Thank you, Captain Winston. For your kindness and for helping with Andrew today."

"It was my pleasure," he said, his deep voice overloud in the silence.

She started for the stairs, yet when she didn't hear the kitchen door open and close again, she turned back to find him watching her.

"Mrs. Prescott . . . I owe you an apology, ma'am. More than one, actually." He took a step toward her. "First, I should've kept my opinion to myself the other day. About the Women's Relief Society auction. It was rude of me to state it aloud. And I'm sorry."

She heard the sincerity in his voice. "Thank you, Captain Winston. However, everyone is entitled to their opinion. I only hope that after you help with the auction, you might discover yours somewhat . . . altered."

He nodded, but the doubt in his expression led her to believe that chance was slim.

He glanced away and when he looked back, she detected a reluctance in him that hadn't been there a moment before. And with no small measure of discomfort, she realized what it portended and sighed inwardly, again feeling as though she'd somewhat contributed to what had happened between them. Or what had *almost* happened.

"Captain Winston, I want to—"

"Mrs. Prescott, I want to—"

They'd spoken at the same time, only to pause simultaneously as well.

He smiled. "Usually I would say ladies first. But I need to offer you an apology, Mrs. Prescott. And I'd appreciate you allowing me to do that."

"All right," she said softly.

"The other night, ma'am . . . I know I made you feel uncomfortable. When I . . . tried to kiss you. I want to say I'm sorry," he added hurriedly. "I had no right to do that. And I want to guarantee you that you have no reason to feel awkward around me. Nor do you have to worry about being safe with me. I appreciate your friendship more than you realize, and your son's." His gaze softened and dropped briefly to Andrew. "I only hope I haven't overstepped my bounds in a way that will prevent our friendship from continuing in the future."

Again hearing his sincerity in his well-chosen words, Aletta shifted Andrew in her arms, the boy growing heavy. "Thank you, Captain, for your kind apology. I accept, of course, and—"

She looked away, embarrassed, feeling almost as if she needed to apologize, too, at least in part. Because she felt guilty for allowing him to think that the longing behind the moment had rested solely with him. Yet she also felt as though her apology would only muddy the waters. And life was murky enough as it was.

"—I'm indebted to you for the kindness you've shown to me and Andrew. Feeling safe in your company, Captain . . . is something I will never worry about."

Relief showed in his expression. "So . . . truce?"

She smiled. "Very much a truce."

She started for the stairs.

"One more thing, if you would . . . a favor, of sorts."

She turned back and studied him for a moment, trying to decipher what that favor might be.

"Since we've reached such an amiable truce, would you please call me Jake? And, likewise, would you allow me to address you by your Christian name, General Prescott?"

She laughed softly. "My name is Aletta . . . Jake."

His pleasure evident in his expression, he gave her a mock salute before closing the door, and she carefully negotiated the stairs up to the bedroom.

Andrew roused when she tried to lay him down, and she busied herself with getting him ready for bed. It was a tad earlier for that than usual, and she hoped he wouldn't fight her on it. She listened as he rattled on about the day's events, his tired voice heightening with excitement.

"Me and Winder had fun, Mama! I know how to kill a pig, boil a pig, and scrape the hair off a pig."

Aletta winced, grateful she'd missed those particular lessons. She reached for a brush and began running it through his dark hair, making a mental note to give him a haircut soon.

"Jake taught me," he continued. "But we held the knife together because it was my first time. He says next time maybe I can do it by myself."

"Jake?" She paused, her grip tightening on the brush. Had Andrew overheard them downstairs just now?

He nodded. "You know . . . the soldier."

"Andrew, you're to call him Captain Winston. Either that or 'sir.' You know children aren't to address adults by their Christian names."

"But he said I could. Today when we were eatin' lunch."

"And I'm saying that you can't. Is that understood?"

He looked at her for a moment then gave a begrudging nod. "He showed me how to build a fire too. And how to sharpen a knife. He knows how to do *lots* of fun stuff."

Grateful for the Captain's attentiveness to her son, Aletta also felt a possessiveness rising inside her. Warren should still be here. Should be the one teaching him all those things. Not a total stranger.

And yet Captain Winston was hardly a total stranger.

"Ouch!" Andrew pulled away. "You're brushin' me too hard."

"Oh, I'm sorry, dear. I didn't realize." She smoothed a hand over his hair and pressed a kiss to the crown of his head.

Gradually, his excitement over the day's activities waned and gave way to fatigue, and she tucked him in on his side of the bed and kissed his forehead, almost regretting it when he slipped off to sleep so quickly.

Because at the moment, silence wasn't a welcome companion.

She retrieved her plate from downstairs in the kitchen and brought it back upstairs and proceeded to eat most of the sausage and tenderloin along with the chow-chow and a slice of cold buttered corn bread. Delicious didn't begin to describe it. As she changed into her nightgown, her gaze dropped briefly to the ever-growing swell of her abdomen, and she wondered whether the child was a boy or a girl. Whether they would have Warren's features and his dark hair—as Andrew did—or her blond hair and fairer skin.

She climbed into bed and pulled up the covers, the sheets cool against her legs.

How long had it been since she'd noticed a man

other than Warren? It wasn't that she'd ceased noticing handsome men after they'd married. She still noticed. But she'd never felt anything for another man since Warren. Not like what she felt with Captain Winston.

Jake.

Thinking about him again brought to mind the way he'd cradled Andrew so gently against his chest, his shirtsleeves rolled up revealing muscular, sun-browned forearms. And the lingering scent of wood smoke mixed with bay rum spice that she'd caught a whiff of when he'd leaned in close.

She squeezed her eyes tight. Noticing those things about him was wrong. No, noticing wasn't wrong. But dwelling on them was. Or it sure felt like it. As was this unexpected longing inside her. It was unsettling. And unwelcome. And with determination, she wrangled her thoughts toward the lists of preparations for the auction, while pushing the others as far from her mind as she could.

Sounds from within the smokehouse next door drew her attention, and she could hear the men working—silent for the most part, and no doubt tired after such a long day. Only occasionally did she hear the low cadence of conversation, then after a while everything went quiet. And she was grateful when sleep finally crept close.

Before she drifted off, an explanation for how

she'd reacted earlier that evening became clearer to her. She was lonely, that's what it was. Lonely and frightened, worried about the future. And she'd been spending quite a bit of time with Jake. Probably too much time, upon reflection. But for the present that was unavoidable, given that Mrs. McGavock had assigned him to help her with the auction.

Between the twilight of wakefulness and dreams, she realized again that what she felt for him was merely her missing Warren. And being lonely. Being frightened and needing reassurance. That was it. It had to be. Sighing, she tucked the covers closer beneath her chin, determined to believe that.

No matter how false the excuses felt.

His thoughts preoccupied, Jake helped with the cleanup outside, then assisted the men as they salted down the pork, packed the joints, and layered the meat on the cooling shelves in the smokehouse. Finally, he headed back to his cabin, his left shoulder aching much as it had in those first days after he'd been shot.

Over the next hour, he hauled water from the spring and heated it in a cast iron pot over the hearth, then filled a large oblong tin tub about halfway. He stripped and got into the tub and poured the warm water over his shoulders and back using another pot he'd found in the cupboard. The heat felt good to his tired muscles. Much as his apology earlier tonight had worked to soothe his guilty conscience. Aletta had forgiven him.

They'd reached a truce. Friends again. Even if what he still felt for her wasn't like what he'd felt for any *friend* before in his life.

He poured several potfuls of warm water over his head, then grabbed the bar of soap and worked up a lather in his hair. While he enjoyed hog killing day, he appreciated the chance to wash away the remnants of it.

Later, the tub emptied and stored again, he sat by the fire in his long johns in the only chair in the room—an ancient rocker made of hickory that would likely outlive him. He picked up today's newspaper that Mrs. McGavock had left for him in the kitchen, reached for his eyeglasses, and—as he did at every chance—scanned the paper for news of the war, advancements made or losses sustained.

He'd been at Carnton for a little over two weeks now, but it felt like much, much longer. He missed being with his regiment and missed doing what he'd been born to do. And wondered if he'd ever be able to do again.

Tempy had replenished his supply of ingredients for the poultices the doctor had prescribed, and he was using them as instructed but still couldn't tell a difference. Yet, with flagging hope, at least fifty times a day, he peered through the rifle sight he kept in his pocket, just in case he happened to—

His gaze snagged on the name *Chattanooga,* and he pulled the newspaper closer.

> The recent Federal victory at Chattanooga, a vital railroad hub, has essentially opened the road to Atlanta for the Federal armies. As earlier reported, following the Battle of Chickamauga in September, Confederate troops besieged those of the Federal in Chattanooga. General Grant took command and the siege has been broken, a thinly stretched army of Confederates being driven from the ridges above the town by an impromptu charge by the Army of the Cumberland.

Jake read on, taking in the words on the page—the descriptions of the fallen, the miscalculations of the Confederate command, the capture of the southern flank on Lookout Mountain—and defeat knifed through him with every syllable. He recalled what Colonel Stratton had told him about Generals Grant and Rosencrans moving southward, but it was the concluding sentence of the article that delivered the final blow.

It's been reported from an unconfirmed source that following the Confederate loss in Chattanooga, General Braxton Bragg—who made a hurried retreat to Dalton, Georgia, after his troops were routed—has resigned. President Davis is said to have immediately accepted his resignation.

Jake felt the air leave his lungs. General Bragg . . . resigned? He bowed his head, his thoughts spinning. *Hurried retreat to Dalton. Troops routed. Thinly stretched army of Confederates.* He slowly lifted his gaze, the flames from the fire in the hearth blurring in his gaze. And here he was at a farm in Franklin assisting a Women's Relief Society.

He rose and tossed the newspaper aside.

Suddenly feeling caged and needing to move, he opened the cabin door and stepped outside onto the porch, welcoming the cold air. He breathed deeply, willing the cool to clear his head. The hoot of an owl carried toward him from some distance away, and he looked in the direction of the darkened house, then to Aletta's window.

Friends. And that's all they ever would be. For so many reasons. Least of which was the war. He determined right then to contact Colonel Stratton and ask him to review his assignment here. Stratton had sent him to Carnton to fulfill a favor of General Bragg's to Colonel McGavock. Since Bragg was no longer in command, perhaps Stratton would rescind the order, consider the obligation met, and then Jake could return to his regiment. Still unable to shoot, of course, but there were other ways he could help them win this war.

He simply needed to convince Stratton of that fact.

CHAPTER 12

His left shoulder complaining, Jake managed to carry another table into the room where Aletta had instructed. He set it down just inside the door. It was still early, but the various rooms of the church building were already brimming with women again, same as the past three days.

Females young and old, with children in tow, had shown up to help with preparations for the auction. So much crinoline. Too much. And the thrum of conversation filled the place. It occurred to him that these women would use more words in a minute than he would likely use in a month of Sundays.

Being the only male in the group, he'd met many if not most of them by now, but had stopped trying to keep track of names after the first four or five. He did recognize Kate Zachary, the widow Aletta had visited last month, and was surprised but pleased to see her among the volunteers. Per Aletta, as soon as the body of Mrs. Zachary's husband was returned, there would be a funeral. Same for the body of Aletta's husband. Jake had offered to help with both in any way he could.

True to Aletta's word, the women had made enormous progress over the past three days. Which, considering all the visiting they did, he found impressive. Some sewed on quilts, others knitted various articles of clothing, all grouped in circles, heads together. And though he still held to his original opinion—it would be far more efficient if everyone simply donated their money to the cause straightaway—he wasn't about to voice it.

"Jake."

He turned to see Aletta looking at him and was glad she couldn't read his thoughts.

"That table goes over there, please." She gestured. "Then would you retrieve the crates of yarn from the back of the wagon? The 'caps and scarves' ladies—those four groups knitting over there—are running low." She flashed him a smile. "Thank you."

She immediately returned to her tasks, not waiting for his response. She was working hard, a bit too hard, if you asked him, for a woman in her condition. He'd encouraged her to take a rest but she'd waved aside the comment, saying she was enjoying it. And granted, it did appear that way. They'd fallen back into a comfortable pattern with each other, which he was grateful for. Still, it wasn't quite as it had been before. He

164

was simply more aware of her. No matter where she was in a room, he knew it. And he sensed she knew it. Which likely accounted for the increased distance she kept between them.

Nothing anyone else would notice, but he did. He positioned the table as she'd indicated, then went outside to get the crates of yarn from the wagon.

He couldn't fault her for keeping that distance either. Like yesterday when she'd placed Andrew squarely between them on the bench seat of the wagon as they'd ridden into town. She hadn't told him until they'd reached her house what they were there for. He shook his head.

Foreclosure.

He'd loaded as much of the smaller furniture and her belongings from the house as he could manage into the back of the wagon and—with Colonel McGavock's approval—had stored it all in one of the outbuildings on the Carnton estate, along with a trunk full of her husband's clothes. Jake was certain Andrew hadn't noticed his mother's silent tears as they'd driven home.

Still, he wished she would've told him about the foreclosure. Not that he could have done anything to stop the bank from repossessing the home, but at least he would've been aware of the situation and could have been more sensitive to her and Andrew's plight.

He stacked the two crates and headed back

inside the church, eager to walk the short distance to the telegraph office later that day to see if Colonel Stratton had responded yet. Surely the man would see his side of things and agree to allow him to return.

Jake delivered the yarn to the "caps and scarves" groups of ladies as requested when he heard a sudden cry. He turned, as did everyone else, and spotted a young woman across the room, a newspaper clutched in her hands. He'd scanned that day's edition an hour earlier and knew the War Department had issued another list of soldiers either killed, wounded, or missing.

He knew that the young woman's relative—be it her husband, brother, or some other kin—hadn't been an officer. When an officer was killed, wounded, or missing, the army, if at all possible, dispatched a rider with personal notification of such in the form of a hand-delivered letter.

"No!" the young woman sobbed and dropped to her knees.

In a blink, every woman in the room stopped what she was doing. Those closest to the young woman surrounded her, kneeling alongside, Aletta among them, a stricken look on her face. The women comforted the grieving woman as she pulled two identical-looking little blond-haired girls close.

Another gasp sounded close by, and a second

woman doubled over in her chair, silent tears tracing her cheeks. She wrapped her arms around herself and around her unborn child, and the deep, mournful keening that rose from her chest caused Jake's own to tighten. The pain in her expression, the depth of her grief and that of the other woman, cut straight through him. And he had to look away.

He'd fought on countless battlefields, had focused his rifle sights on a man's chest then pulled the trigger. He'd seen boys who would never reach manhood cut down by cannon fodder or gutted with a bayonet. He'd watched soldiers struggle to take their last breaths, their bloodied chests rising and falling with the effort. He'd walked among the corpses after battle, the stench of gunpowder and death heavy in the air, and he'd felt compassion, grief, and had accorded them a soldier's respect and honor. And on more than one occasion, back in his tent, he'd wept bitter tears beneath the weight and horror of it all. But this . . .

These women were defenseless. They weren't on the battlefield. They weren't brandishing weapons or—

"Jake?"

Hearing her voice, he turned.

"Would you please make the wagon ready and escort Mrs. Buckner and her two young daughters home? They live a good ways from town and

I don't want them to have to walk all that way back."

He nodded, grateful for a task. "Of course I will."

"As well as Mrs. Hunter," Aletta continued. "Alice lives here in town and this is their first—" Her voice caught. "First child," she finished in a whisper, her voice failing.

His throat constricted, making it difficult to speak. "I'll make certain they get home safely, Aletta."

"That would be much appreciated. Some of the other ladies will accompany them, too, I'm sure. And they're already making plans for meals. So please make certain there's room in the back of the wagon for them."

He nodded. "I'll make sure both ladies have on hand what they need for a few days before I head back here."

Chin trembling, she nodded.

He walked to the door, then turned back, not as surprised as he would've been before spending time with these women to see the groups who had been knitting and sewing and chatting together only moments earlier now huddled together again. But this time with heads bowed, lips moving silently as whispered prayers rose from around the room.

How could he ever have thought that women could be shielded from war's cruelties? That they weren't strong enough to bear up beneath the weight of it? Granted, he would never wish to be fighting side by side with them on the battlefield.

But these women were fighting nonetheless. On a battlefield all their own.

Aletta pulled three loaves of hot pumpkin bread from the oven, mentally ticking off the final item on her menu that awaited Mrs. McGavock's approval before the auction officially began on the seventeenth of December, only eleven days hence. But this recipe was a tried-and-true Prescott family recipe, so she'd intentionally saved it for last.

She caught a flash of movement outside the window and spotted Andrew and Winder running full tilt from the barn toward the house. Following their lunch break from studies—which almost always included a trip to the barn—they would enter the house through the kitchen to see if there was anything of interest, so she prepared for the door to fly open. Which it did only seconds later.

"Somethin' smells good in here, Mama!" Andrew ran up to the counter, cheeks flushed, breath coming hard.

"Can we have some, Mrs. Prescott?" Winder leaned close, eyeing the warm pumpkin bread.

"Thank you, Andrew. And yes, Winder, you may both have a slice. After you wash your hands from all that playing with the kittens."

They made a beeline for the washbasin, each boy boasting about how much pumpkin bread he could eat without regurgitating it. Aletta shook her head but had to smile. Where did boys get these ideas? Then her smile faded.

Although she was grateful for this job—not only for the money it provided, but for a safe place for them to live in the interim—she had begun to dread the day coming soon enough when she and Andrew would have to pack up and leave and find somewhere else to live.

She'd heard of special homes in other cities that specifically accommodated only widows and orphans, and where everyone shared in the running of the place. And it had sounded so promising. But after checking with several sources, she'd learned that Nashville didn't have one of those homes. Which was unfortunate. She knew so many women and children, herself and Andrew included, who would have benefited from it.

Losing the house to foreclosure last week had been far more painful than she'd imagined. And even now the memory of walking through each of the rooms for the last time brought a reminiscence she didn't wish to indulge. All of this cooking and baking, the organization required for the auction, had been a godsend during this time of uncertainty.

All the to-dos for the upcoming event had

helped occupy her thoughts and her time. And her grief. Looking back over the last two years since Warren first left to fight in the war, she knew now that she'd been grieving his absence and his possible death since the very beginning.

She fed both boys a thick slice of warm, buttered pumpkin bread, then, knowing them well, cut second slices to cool while they were devouring their first. She stopped to rub the ache in her lower back, grateful she hadn't experienced any more episodes like the one the day of the hog killing. Only six weeks or so until her baby was due—her approximation aided by knowing, within a handful of days, when she had conceived—and the precious child was steadily growing. Which meant she was too.

Needing more wood for the stove, she threw her shawl around her shoulders and stepped outside the back door. Where yesterday's wood bin had been nearly empty, today it was full.

Jake, she knew. Because she'd seen him chopping wood behind the barn. Shot in the shoulder . . . If a man could chop wood, shouldn't he be able to shoot and fight as well?

Feeling guilty for not being more grateful for the wood, and for all he'd done over the past few days to help with activities at the church—not to mention assisting her in moving belongings from her house—she gathered an armful and carried it back inside.

She'd made an effort to be alone with him as little as possible in recent days, which hadn't been that difficult with Tempy and the boys around. And based on his behavior toward her, she felt certain that whatever momentary attraction he'd felt toward her had passed. Not surprising, looking the way she did. And her feelings for him truly were those of friendship.

She saw that now, having had time to parse her sentimentalities. Because enjoying someone's company and looking forward to being with them wasn't the same as being attracted to them.

CHAPTER 13

The next evening, Aletta practically had to drag herself out to the barn to work on the nativity. She was nearly finished with the project and eager to get it done. But after baking and cooking all day, even with the other hired cooks assisting, she could scarcely scrape up the energy.

She lit two lanterns, knowing that once she got started, momentum for seeing the job done well would carry her forward. That, and the second cup of coffee she'd had with dinner.

She surveyed the remaining work. Once she finished constructing the last side of the booth, she would require Jake's help again from there on out. Which included attaching the star to the top. And she'd promised both Andrew and Winder that they could help with that final step. But for now . . .

She retrieved her father's carpenter's pouch, the worn leather supple and familiar, and pulled out the mallet and the remaining nails and set to work. After a while, Andrew joined her with a cup of hot cocoa in hand.

"It's for you from Miss Tempy."

Aletta stood and stretched from side to side, then accepted the offered treat. She started to take a drink, then paused and looked back at him, doing her best to make her frown look real. "If it's for me, then why is half of it gone?"

He grinned. "I didn't want to spill any on the way so I drank a little."

She laughed and took a sip. Delicious as usual. She'd finally managed to watch Tempy mixing a batch one day and had learned the woman's secret—a little salt and vanilla. And, of course, a generous amount of cream.

"Are we ready to hang the star yet, Mama?"

"Almost. But I'm to the point now where I'm going to need some help putting it all together."

He jumped up. "I'll help."

She tousled his hair. "I appreciate that. But I think you and I *might* require a third person for this next part."

Just then Aletta looked over to see Jake walking from the house, past the barn and toward his cabin.

"Captain Winston!" she called.

He turned, gave a quick wave, and headed in their direction. "Evening, Aletta." He knelt and gave Andrew a playful poke in the tummy. "Hey, buddy, how you doing?"

"I'm good, Ja—" Andrew cut his eyes in her direction. "I mean . . . Captain Winston, sir. You

174

want some cocoa? Tempy made some just now."

Jake smiled. "That sounds good, thank you."

Aletta caught her son's gaze, appreciating how he'd corrected his mistake. "Do you plan on drinking half of the Captain's too?"

With an impish grin, Andrew darted back to the kitchen.

"Fine boy you've got there, Aletta."

"Thank you. I think I'll keep him."

"With good reason."

Jake eyed the booth lying in pieces on the barn floor beside the manger, and knelt to examine her work. "Very impressive. Your father taught you well."

"I only wish I'd learned how to carve like he could. He would've taught me, but I didn't consider it important enough at the time."

He ran a hand over the manger and looked up at her, a mischievous gleam in his eyes. "It's never too late to learn something new."

"I've got yours, Captain Winston!"

They looked up to see Andrew slowly walking toward them, his attention homed in on the cup in his hands.

Captain Winston took the cup from him but eyed it suspiciously. "Tell me now . . . how much of mine did you drink?"

Andrew grinned. "Not as much as Mama's."

They all laughed, and Aletta packed up the tools in her father's pouch, having had enough

175

for one day. As they walked back to the house, Andrew pointed toward the sky.

"Hey, Mama! There's the Big Dipper! Just like Papa showed me."

Aletta looked up, remembering the night Warren had first pointed out that constellation to him. "Yes, and the Big Dipper is part of . . . what? Do you remember?"

Andrew squinted. "The bear!"

"That's right! And do you see it too?" She knelt beside him. "Follow the invisible line down my arm to where I'm pointing."

Seconds passed.

"I see it! Do you see the bear too, Captain Winston?" Andrew asked.

When Jake didn't answer immediately, Aletta looked up to see him searching the night sky. And she almost wondered if he couldn't locate the constellation.

"Anybody can see it if they know where to look," he finally responded. "It's right up there. Just like it's supposed to be."

"Papa told me if you ever get lost, the stars can get you home."

Jake nodded. "That's right. Your papa was a very smart man."

"And he promised me a train for Christmas. Which isn't long from now!"

Aletta didn't say anything but could feel Jake's attention shift in her direction. "Remember what

I said about Santa this year, Andrew. He's going to be very busy. So we must be grateful for whatever gift is under the tree for us."

"Yes, ma'am." Then Andrew leaned toward Jake. "But mine's gonna be a train," he whispered.

Jake only smiled. "I'll bid you two good evening. Sleep well, Andrew." He ruffled the boy's hair. "And, Aletta, I'll see you tomorrow and we'll put the finishing touches on your masterpiece."

"Thank you, Jake. And good evening."

Later as she readied for bed, Andrew already asleep, Aletta moved to the window to blow out the oil lamp when the warm glow from the window of the cabin just beyond the smokehouse drew her attention. She spotted Jake sitting before the fireplace reading, it looked like. Or perhaps he was sketching in that notebook of his. She'd glimpsed one of his drawings before. That of a grove of trees, and it was quite good.

He stood and stretched, then turned toward the window. And stilled. She hurriedly blew out the flame of the oil lamp, but the flame sputtered—and returned to life. Too late, he'd seen her.

He moved closer to the window and waved. Smiling despite herself, Aletta pressed her palm flat against the cool pane of glass. Strange, how a man she'd met scarcely a month ago could make her feel so much less alone.

Trying a second time, she successfully extinguished the oil lamp and crawled into bed beside Andrew and slept more soundly than she had in weeks.

CHAPTER 14

"You must admit, Jake, that at the start you didn't think I'd be able to do this."

"That is absolutely—" Jake started to protest but hesitated, looking from her to the fully assembled nativity situated in the side yard by the winter garden. "The uncontested truth."

She beamed and turned again to admire her handiwork, and with good reason.

"You should be very proud of yourself, Aletta."

She nodded. "I am."

"And I" he winced—"should be somewhat ashamed."

"Yes, you should be." She playfully narrowed her eyes. "But truly, I couldn't have built this without your help. So thank you."

He offered a salute. "My pleasure, General Prescott."

She began picking up the tools scattered in the yard and placing them back in the bucket. He did likewise. He hadn't heard back from Colonel Stratton yet in regard to his returning to the regiment, which was answer enough in itself, Jake guessed.

He looked over at her. "So who's your first Mary and Joseph?"

"Hattie and Andrew. Winder wanted to be the first Joseph, until he found out his sister was going to be Mary."

Jake gave her a look. "Wise boy. Do you have a baby Jesus yet?"

"Baby Jesus is being sewn together at the church as we speak." She looked over. "You must admit, Jake, having seen what those women can do over the last few days, that it's impressive. They've knitted almost six hundred scarves, caps, and pairs of gloves between them for the soldiers. And seven quilts for the auction. And they're still knitting and sewing."

"I admit, they're a far more productive group than I thought they'd be. And talkative. Especially that Mrs. Peterson." The woman had to be eighty if she was a day, and she'd all but talked him to death on more than one occasion.

Aletta chuckled, shaking her head. "Yes, Mrs. Peterson is most definitely a handful. But to be her age and have that energy. She's quite the—" She gasped, wincing as she pressed a hand to her abdomen.

"Aletta!" Jake was by her side in an instant. "Are you all right?"

She took several deep breaths. "Yes . . ." She gripped his arm, her complexion flushed, despite the chill of December. "I'm fine. But perhaps I should sit down for a moment or two."

Holding her hand and with his arm about her waist, he led her to a bench a few feet away beneath an osage orange tree. A hedge of hydrangea provided shelter from the wind and he sat down beside her.

"Better?" he asked.

Eyes closed, she breathed through pursed lips. "Mmm-hmm . . . or I will be."

His gaze dropped to her hand, so small and pale by comparison, still tucked in his, then moved to the swell of her belly where her unborn child lay nestled within. A sense of protectiveness rose up inside him, and he prayed as he sat there beside her that all would be well for her, for her baby. For little Andrew too. And he couldn't deny—no matter how he tried, no matter how he told himself it wasn't wise—that he wished there was a place for him in her life. Their lives.

Finally, she exhaled and opened her eyes, their blue so vibrant and alive. "Well, that was exciting." She laughed softly.

"Is . . . everything proceeding as it should? With . . . the baby?"

The smile in her eyes deepened. "Yes, everything is fine. It's normal to have these pains. I had the same with Andrew."

"And how many weeks are left before the baby is expected?"

"Five, at least. Andrew came three weeks early but I'd been sick with him. The doctor said that had a lot to do with it. And as you can see, I'm fit as a fiddle now." She shrugged. "A very big fiddle."

He smiled at the look on her face. "I can't imagine you being any more beautiful than you are right now, Aletta. You . . . shine from the inside out."

She shook her head. "That's probably just perspiration from building the nativity."

They laughed, then she looked down at her hand still tucked in his. She gently started to pull away, but he brought her hand to his lips and kissed it. Once, twice, her skin like silk. Her gaze lowered from his eyes to his mouth, and the simple gesture sent something akin to a thunderbolt through him. There'd been plenty of times when he'd looked at her and wished he'd earned the liberty to kiss her, to hold her close. But never more so than right at that moment. As though she'd read his thoughts, her cheeks flushed crimson.

Jake traced a feather path with his thumb across her lower lip, and her mouth opened slightly. He told himself to move slowly where this woman was concerned. But when she closed her eyes, that was all the answer he needed.

He kissed her gently at first, her mouth softer, sweeter than he'd imagined. But when a soft sigh rose in her throat, he drew her closer and she slipped her arms around his neck. He deepened the kiss, weaving his hands into her hair and—

"Mama! We're here to help with the star!"

Jake drew back slightly and broke the kiss, hearing the boys barreling in their direction. Aletta looked up at him and smiled, and whatever determination he'd had to move slowly where she was concerned vanished completely.

"Mama?" Andrew called.

"I'm coming," she answered and stood, smoothing the sides of her hair then the front of her dress. Jake rose along with her and reached over and tucked a wayward curl back into place, then kissed her on the forehead.

They joined the boys, who each gave a loud whoop as Aletta pulled the star from a crate.

"Captain Winston will help you each up there." She smiled. "Then I'll hand the star to you and you can put it into place together!"

Jake lifted the two boys to the top of the booth, the structure sturdy enough to hold far more weight than that. When this woman built something, she built it to last.

He stayed close as she directed them on positioning the wooden star atop the three-sided booth, and he couldn't help but admire her, both as a carpenter—and as a woman.

"Very nicely done!" She grinned up at the boys. "Now be careful climbing down."

But climbing down wasn't their plan. Clearly seeing what the boys intended, Jake gestured to Andrew first—and caught him as he jumped down. Then did the same with Winder.

The front door opened and Miss Clouston, the nanny, stepped out. "Well done, Mrs. Prescott! Captain Winston!" The woman beamed. "And you too, boys! Now you two come back inside and let's get to work so you'll have time to play after your studies."

The boys obeyed and as Jake continued picking up tools, he heard the sound of horse's hooves and spotted a rider coming up the road. But he couldn't make out the precise definition.

Aletta turned, her gaze trailing his. And she went perfectly still.

She slowly set the bucket down and walked to the gate. Jake followed. Only when the rider grew close did he realize who it was.

The Confederate soldier dismounted and walked as far as the gate. "A letter from the War Department. For a Mrs. Warren Prescott."

Aletta stared at the envelope trembling in her hand, feeling as though her world had turned inside out. Only from a distance did she hear the retreat of horse's hooves and feel Jake's presence beside her.

She looked up at him and saw in his expression the same contorted jumble of emotions that described what she was feeling at that very moment. She slipped a forefinger beneath the flap, which lifted with surprising ease.

She withdrew the letter, a wordless utterance rising from deep inside her as her gaze flew over the address at the top, the date, the opening salutation and went to the first sentence. *It is with deep regret over the needless pain that was caused you but also with fresh hope that I write to inform you that your husband, Warren, who was thought to have been mortally wounded in battle, is indeed very much alive and is—*

Aletta felt her knees about to buckle. She reached out to grab hold of something solid, and Jake's arm came about her waist. She leaned into his strength, her own hand shaking so badly she could scarcely hold the letter.

She blinked as the words on the page blurred in her vision, a fury of joy, disbelief, dread, and guilt pounding through her veins. "He's alive," she whispered, looking up at him. "Warren is alive."

CHAPTER 15

Seated beside Jake in the wagon as it jostled and jolted over the rutted dirt road, Aletta was aware of every time their bodies touched. Even as she thanked God that Warren was alive— *her husband was alive!*—she could still feel Jake's lips on hers, could feel the tender urgency in his kiss, and his strong arms holding her close.

Jake sat silent beside her on the bench seat, reins held taut, focus forward, expression cast in stone.

"Thank you," she said softly, "for driving me to the hospital."

He nodded, his jaw firming. "I'll be with you. Every step of the way. If you want me to."

The forced control in his voice brought tears to her eyes. Why had she allowed herself to grow so close to him? And so soon after Warren's death? She'd known it wasn't wise. And yet she'd done it anyway. And now she was reaping the bittersweet harvest of that decision.

As soon as they entered the hospital in Thompson's Station, Aletta realized that though she'd thought she knew the horrors of war, she'd only known the outer hell. Men lined the hallway, some on cots, most on the wood floor, groaning in pain, crying, begging for medication, some whispering in ragged pleas for the comfort of their mothers. And, to a man, everyone she saw had lost an arm or a leg. Or both.

"It's going to be all right," Jake whispered beside her. "Let's speak with the nurse over here."

She nodded and followed, grateful to him for taking charge.

She hadn't told Andrew where she was going, and it had helped that Mrs. McGavock had agreed with her decision. Best learn what the situation was first, then tell Andrew once she was better equipped to answer his questions. But one blessed fact was certain . . .

Her children would grow up knowing their father.

"This is Second Lieutenant Warren Prescott's wife," Jake said to the nurse. "Here to see her husband."

The nurse checked a roster then nodded. "Come with me, please."

Aletta followed, so grateful, so nervous, her heart breaking in two places at once, all while grieving over what Warren must have endured in recent weeks. Mindful of the soldiers lying in the corridor, she watched where she stepped.

The nurse opened the door to a dormitory-style room with beds lined up one after the other. The nurse led them down the narrow center aisle, and Aletta searched each bruised and bandaged face staring back at her, looking for his. The nurse stopped at the foot of a bed, checked the file hanging by a string, then nodded.

"Your husband was severely wounded, Mrs. Prescott. But he *is* going to live. The medical records state he hasn't regained consciousness since being injured. For certain, he hasn't been conscious since coming to us. Yet the doctors believe he will be very soon."

Listening, Aletta moved to the side of the bed and looked at her husband in it. She tried not to cry but couldn't help it. The bedcovers were pressed flat where his lower right leg had once been. Bandages covered his scalp and part of his face, and what wasn't bandaged was marred with swollen cuts and bruises.

"Oftentimes after such trauma," the nurse continued, her voice hushed, "the body needs rest, so the brain will command that it sleep."

"Like a coma," Aletta whispered, reaching for Warren's hand while keenly aware of Jake watching from only feet away.

"Yes, very similar. Only, your husband isn't in that deep of a sleep. He has been stirring. Perhaps the sound of your voice will bring him back. That's often the case in such situations. I'll

188

be in the hallway tending other patients should you need anything."

Aletta nodded, then looked back at Jake and drew strength from his steady gaze. "I'm so sorry," she wanted to say to him. But couldn't. Because part of her wasn't sorry. This was her husband, the father of her children, her companion, her lover, her closest friend, her life lying in this bed.

"Talk to him," Jake whispered, his own voice heavy with emotion.

Aletta leaned closer, her belly brushing against the bed. "Warren," she whispered, gently squeezing his hand. "Wake up, my love. Wake up."

He didn't move.

She searched his bandaged face and placed a gentle hand on his arm. "Andrew is well and is looking forward to seeing you. And our child I'm carrying is doing well too." Tears slipped down her cheeks. "I wrote you letters. Several, actually." She laughed softly. "Did you—"

His eyes fluttered open, and her breath caught. She leaned even closer so that he could see her, mindful not to put any weight on his body. "I'm here," she whispered. "And you're going to be all right."

He looked at her then, blinking as if trying to focus, and squeezed her hand tight. A sound rose from within his chest and a tear trailed down his temple. Aletta searched his gaze and felt a similar cry rising up from within her even as she squeezed his hand back. She couldn't stem the tears and didn't even try. She only looked into his eyes and nodded. And knew.

She looked back at Jake, not certain her voice would hold. "This isn't my husband," she managed, her lungs betraying her. "This is . . . Emmett Zachary."

CHAPTER 16

"Emmett Zachary?" Jake repeated, uncertain if he'd heard her corrcctly. But her expression, filled with heartrending anguish, confusion, and—could it be—a glimmer of relief, told him he had, then told him far more.

She bowed her head, her breath coming hard, same as that of the wounded soldier in the bed. After a moment, she lifted her gaze and tenderly laid a hand on the man's bandaged forehead.

"Shhh," she whispered through tears. "It's all right, Emmett. Your Kate will be overjoyed to see you. To know you're alive."

Zachary sucked in a breath, his body shuddering. He attempted to speak but his voice came out raspy from disuse, the words scarcely intelligible.

"You don't have to talk right now," she said softly. "It's all right."

But he shook his head, determination in his eyes. She reached for a cup of water and a cloth on the bedside table and held it to his lips. He drank, coughing as he did, water running down

191

his chin. She dabbed it away with the cloth and leaned closer.

"I'm s—" His voice broke. Fresh tears slid down his temples. "—sorry . . . Mrs. Prescott."

She took his hand in both of hers and a moment passed before she spoke. "Were you with him? Were you with Warren when he . . ." Her voice faded.

The answer showed clearly in Zachary's eyes even before his slow, single nod. Then he squeezed his eyes tight as though reliving the awful memory, and she bowed her head, her shoulders gently shaking.

Jake felt a coolness on his cheek but didn't bother wiping the tears away.

Mrs. McGavock stared, unblinking, her face pale. "So you're certain then, Mrs. Prescott?" she whispered. "There's not a chance that another mistake has been made? That—"

"No, ma'am." Aletta shook her head. "We're certain."

Aletta felt as though she couldn't possibly have any tears left in her, yet they kept coming. She was weary beyond comprehension. Her eyes ached and her head throbbed. It seemed like this day might go on forever. She looked over at Jake seated on the settee opposite hers, and he seemed to understand her unspoken request.

He leaned forward. "After visiting with Corporal

Zachary earlier today, Mrs. McGavock, it became clear what happened. Second Lieutenant Prescott—" He paused. "Mrs. Prescott's husband, Warren, was killed on the sixteenth of October when his division came under fire from a regiment of Federal troops outside Nashville. They were outnumbered ten to one. Zachary saw the Second Lieutenant get hit. Multiple times." His voice softened. "He said that Mrs. Prescott's husband was dead before he hit the ground."

Aletta bowed her head, grateful to have learned that Warren hadn't suffered. That his death had been swift.

"The Federal army was closing in," Jake continued. "So our troops had to retreat, which meant leaving behind those who'd fallen. It was several days before the ambulance corps was finally able to get back in and collect the bodies. But the Second Lieutenant couldn't be properly identified—until they found a letter in the pocket of his trousers. It was addressed to Mrs. Emmett Zachary, so—"

"They made the assumption," Mrs. McGavock finished for him. "But why was he carrying a letter for Mrs. Zachary? And further, does the woman know yet that her husband is alive?"

"Yes, ma'am, she does," Jake answered. "We went straight to Mrs. Zachary's house after we left the hospital. As for Warren Prescott having a letter addressed to her . . . we wondered the very same thing." He paused and looked at Aletta.

She took a breath. "As it turns out, Mr. Zachary can't read or write. He would dictate his letters home to Warren, then Warren would address the envelopes and mail them. Mr. Zachary said that Warren had gotten leave to go into town to mail both his letter and Warren's the next day. So . . ."

Mrs. McGavock briefly closed her eyes. "So your husband was carrying both letters. But that doesn't account for what happened to the letter he'd written to you, and why that wasn't found. And why they mistakenly identified Emmett Zachary as your husband."

"Actually—" Jake looked from Aletta to Mrs. McGavock. "That was made clear as well. Zachary shared that he'd seen Second Lieutenant Prescott put a bundle of envelopes in his front coat pocket that morning. So when the Lieutenant got shot, Zachary stopped. The Corporal said that even though he didn't think anyone could live through such an assault, he wanted to be certain the wound was fatal. He also wanted to close Prescott's eyes." Jake's voice went soft. "Then he grabbed the letters and retreated with the others. Zachary said he intended to mail the letter to his wife, which he thought was in the bundle. But his division was ordered south to Chattanooga and they never met a mail wagon on the way. So later, when Corporal Zachary was wounded and brought in—"

"They found the bundle of letters and once again assumed." Mrs. McGavock sighed.

Jake nodded. "Which you can see how they could. More than once I've walked battlefields where dozens of bodies couldn't be identified. It's not at all uncommon."

Aletta drew in a breath. "With the extent of Corporal Zachary's injuries, even I didn't realize it wasn't Warren until the man opened his eyes. They favored each other in build and in coloring. Almost could have been brothers."

The *tick-tock* of a clock marked off the seconds somewhere behind her.

Mrs. McGavock rose from her chair and moved to sit beside Aletta on the settee. "I'm so sorry for your loss, my dear. Not only once, but for a second time."

Mrs. McGavock drew her into an embrace and Aletta briefly closed her eyes. When she opened them, she saw Jake staring at her, the same mixture of guilt and relief in his expression that she felt in her own.

After a moment, Mrs. McGavock drew back. "But wait . . . if Mr. Zachary had a bundle of letters with him, then that means—"

Aletta reached into her reticule and withdrew the bloodstained envelopes tied with twine. "These are the recent letters I'd written to him." She bit her lower lip. "And the last letter he wrote to me."

She smoothed a trembling hand over the familiar handwriting on the envelope, still sealed and unread.

Later that evening, Aletta sat on the edge of the bed holding the envelope, Andrew finally quieted and asleep beside her. She slid her forefinger beneath the sealed flap of the envelope and withdrew a single sheet of paper.

She started to unfold it, then paused and closed her eyes, not to whisper a prayer but simply to . . . be still. And to recall happier memories of Warren than the ones today had given her.

She turned her thoughts back, back, back . . . like thumbing through the pages of a well-loved book. And after a moment, she could see him. Warren's face so clear in her mind, his smile, the joy lighting his eyes when he would toss Andrew high in the air and catch him and hold him close. She could see his handsome features in the soft glow of lamplight as he'd sat by the hearth reading at night before they retired to bed.

Emmett Zachary hadn't been surprised to find her with child, so at least she knew that Warren had gotten that letter she'd written. He'd known they were going to have another child.

She let out a sigh, opened her eyes, and unfolded the letter. Her gaze went first to the date—9 October, 1863, almost two months ago today—then to the familiar script.

My dearest Lettie,

This will be brief, but I trust that after my last three ramblings earlier this past month, you may find this discovery more of a relief than a disappointment.

Three rambling letters . . . that she'd never received. She read on.

The sun is rising, and we'll soon break camp. I wish you were here, Lettie, right now, only for a moment, to share the dawn with me. Or even more, I wish I were there. I miss you and Andrew more than I thought possible, and I'd already set that expectation mighty high.

I hope you and the baby are well. It pains me more than I can say not to be with you during this time. I've recalled, on more than one occasion, the conversations we had about this war before I left. And while I still believe, more than ever, in our cause, I do believe you were right, my dearest. That the cost, to both sides, will be greater and leave a far deeper and more lasting wound than anyone anticipated at the outset. I could never have imagined the horrors and indecencies I have witnessed over these long months during our separation. And I wonder if our nation will ever fully heal from this wound that we have inflicted upon ourselves.

If God is gracious enough to hear my prayers, and I believe he is and does, then may he answer them and see me through this journey and back to you and Andrew. And to our precious child yet to be born.

Though I am not so far from you in the span of distance, I am yet another world away. But no matter where I am, my love, know that I carry your love inside me and that I am holding you close even now, recalling the sweet smell of your hair, the warmth of your smile, and the melody of your laughter. I cherish you more than words can say, and eagerly await the day our family will be joined together once again.

As ever, your faithful and loving husband,

Warren

Aletta read the missive again and again, her tears moistening the bottom of the page. Then she pulled back the bedcovers, removed her boots, and, still fully clothed, slipped between the sheets. She extinguished the lamp, letter still in hand, and lay unmoving in the darkness, grieving the love she'd lost with Warren's passing, for the second time. And also the seed of what might have been love, one day, with Jake.

Because if today had shown her anything, it had shown her she wasn't strong enough to go through this again. To love someone and lose them. She didn't want to be that strong. And when Jake returned to his regiment, which he undoubtedly would following the auction, there were no assurances that he would come home. On the contrary. The growing number of widows helping with the auction who filled the church every day attested to that.

No matter where I am, my love, know that I carry your love inside me . . .

Love outlasted this life and carried on into the next. She believed that with all her heart. But that was just it. She'd given her heart once, and now it felt as though half of it had been ripped from her chest—all over again. Did she knowingly want to open herself to that kind of pain a second time?

She turned onto her side, the baby moving within her as she did, and stared into the white-hot embers of the fire in the hearth, listening to the sharp crackle and pop of the wood as it succumbed, without a choice, to the flame.

CHAPTER 17

Jake awakened early the next morning, eager to see Aletta. With everything that had happened yesterday and her retiring earlier than usual last night, they hadn't had time to talk, just the two of them, about what had happened once the initial shock had worn off.

He'd been so proud of her. The way she'd handled the discovery at the hospital with such graceful strength, how she'd comforted Emmett Zachary even though her own heart was clearly breaking. The way she'd spoken to the other wounded soldiers as they'd left the hospital, tenderly touching a shoulder here, wiping a brow there. She'd insisted they go immediately to Kate Zachary's house so that the woman's grief could be turned to joy. And it had been.

On their way back to Carnton, Aletta had asked him to drive by her former home in town. He'd stopped the wagon out front, and she'd simply stared at the house for the longest time, silent tears falling. Then, giving a soft nod, she'd turned and faced forward, the resolution in her spirit nearly tangible.

He closed the cabin door behind him, and as he neared the house, he spotted her through one of the kitchen windows and paused. She was cutting Andrew's hair. And from the looks of things, the boy was talking a mile a minute.

He watched mother and son for a moment, so grateful that God had brought him to Carnton, and so honored that a woman as fine as Aletta not only would look twice at a man like him, but would open herself up to him. Maybe even entrust her heart to him. A heart he would guard and cherish, and solemnly vow before God Almighty never to disappoint.

But one thing remained . . .

He needed to tell her the truth about his injury. The bullet he'd taken in the shoulder was nothing compared to his other wound, and she had a right to know.

His close-up vision hadn't changed in recent weeks. Which was good news, according to what the army doc had said. Because if his close-up vision hadn't changed by now, it likely wouldn't. But the bad news . . . He could no more see through that rifle sight today than he could a month ago.

Movement from inside the kitchen drew his attention, and he spotted Andrew waving at him. Jake opened the kitchen door and stepped inside, and he felt a slight pang in his chest at the way the boy's eyes lit.

"Hey, Captain Winston! I'm learnin' more about stars in class! Miss Clouston, she gave me this to read." Andrew held up a book with pictures of stars on the front, his grin spreading from ear to ear. "Come spring, me and Winder, we're gonna have us a sleep out in the field and look up at the stars all night long."

Jake nodded. "That sounds like a fine plan." He finally managed to catch Aletta's gaze, though it took a bit of work. "Morning, Aletta," he said softly.

"Good morning." She offered him a smile that didn't quite reach her eyes, and he wondered if she hadn't slept well. Understandable, if that was the case.

He gestured to a bowl of eggs. "Want me to get breakfast started?"

She shook her head. "You don't have to do that. I'm about done here with Andrew."

"Mama, how come Captain Winston's hair can touch his collar and mine can't?"

Jake eyed her, wondering how she was going to respond.

"Because Captain Winston is a grown man, Andrew. And grown men can decide for themselves how long they want their hair to be."

Andrew frowned as he climbed down from the stool. "But boys with mamas can't?"

Jake could tell Aletta was trying not to smile. "That's right. Once you're older, then you can decide for yourself how long you want your hair to be."

Andrew seemed to let that settle in, then turned to Jake. "Has your mama died, Captain Winston?"

Jake nodded. "Yes, Andrew. She has."

"Your papa too?"

"Yes," he answered softly. "And my only brother."

"Do you miss 'em?"

"Every day."

"I miss my papa too." Andrew bowed his head.

Jake knelt beside him. "You know, as the years have passed, I can still feel my family with me. In here." Jake touched the place over his heart. "Just like you'll do with your papa . . . who was a very wise and good man. And you'll grow up to be just like him someday."

Without warning, Andrew launched himself at him, and Jake hugged him close, the little boy's arms around his neck about the best thing he could ever remember feeling.

"It's going to be okay, buddy."

"You promise?" Andrew whispered against his neck.

"I promise," Jake whispered back, praying he could be part of keeping that promise in the boy's life. And in his mother's. He caught Aletta's gaze and saw tears rising to her eyes. He saw something else there too. Something he couldn't define but that didn't feel particularly comfortable to him.

"Can I go check on the kittens, Mama?"

Aletta nodded. "You may. But don't stay long. Breakfast will be ready soon. And wear your coat!"

Andrew grabbed his coat from the peg in the hallway, and Jake was grateful for the chance to talk with Aletta privately. Then Tempy entered the kitchen carrying a pail of fresh milk.

"Mornin', Captain Winston!" Tempy grinned. "Oh, Andrew. Look at your hair! So handsome!"

Andrew smiled and ducked his head. "Mama did it."

"Well, maybe your sweet mama could get ahold of the Captain's hair too."

Jake curbed his smile. "I beg your pardon?"

Tempy eyed him as Andrew shot out the door. "You cut off that hairy old beard, but you ain't done nothin' yet with that hair." She set the pail of milk on a table. "We got that auction comin' up and you bein' the only soldier and all . . . You might wanna tidy up a bit. Sit on down on that stool and let Missus Prescott fix you up."

Accustomed to Tempy's teasing, Jake looked over at Aletta to get her take on the conversation. But her eyes held the same reservation from moments before. Only this time, the pain—no, the dread—in them gave him an uneasy feeling. Especially when she looked away.

"You know, Tempy, I think you're right." He sat down on the stool, beginning to feel as though the older woman was giving him a little help. "I could probably stand some tidying up. If you don't mind . . . Mrs. Prescott," he said softly.

Aletta looked at him as though she suspected his primary reason for being on that stool was to be close to her. And if that's what she was thinking, she would've been right.

She draped a cloth around his shoulders and started clipping.

"Oh!" Tempy let out a sigh. "I forgot to get somethin' from the spring house. I'll be back directly. I'd forget my own head if God hadn't attached it for me," she murmured, closing the kitchen door behind her.

Jake smiled to himself. Yep, Tempy was definitely helping him out.

He watched Aletta, willing her to look at him, and acutely aware of how close they were, and of her body. Namely, of her belly pressing up against him.

"Did you sleep all right last night?" he finally asked.

She gave a little shrug, then nodded, the snip of the scissors filling the silence.

"Yesterday was a hard day," he tried again, wishing she'd open up to him.

But nothing.

She moved to the other side, then around

behind him, her hands in his hair nothing short of intoxicating. Then he felt something push him hard in the back and he turned around.

"What was that?"

"Jake, be careful! I have scissors in my hand!"

"But . . . I felt something."

She sighed, the ghost of a smile—and maybe embarrassment—touching her lips. "That was the baby."

He looked from her face to her belly then back again. "*That* was the baby?"

She laughed, despite looking like she wished she hadn't. "You've never felt a baby move inside a woman's womb."

"I believe that goes without saying, Aletta."

She smiled then, the natural response he'd grown accustomed to seeing, and looked at him for a moment. She laid the scissors aside. "Give me your hand."

Never one to be shy, Jake hesitated for a second, then did as she asked.

She placed his hand toward the top of her belly then covered it with hers before gently pressing her belly in on the other side. Then Jake felt it—movement beneath the palm of his hand. Not a quick punch like before. But a gentle pressure that moved across his palm and took his breath along with it.

He looked up at Aletta, her eyes bright even as his blurred.

"That's—"

"Life," she whispered.

He started to take his hand away, but she held it there.

"Wait." She briefly closed her eyes. "I think he—or she—is starting to turn."

Jake's mouth slipped open, and he stared at her belly as he not only felt but *saw* the child within her moving. He sat speechless until she finally lifted her hand.

He drew his hand away and looked up at her, not sure his voice would hold. "Thank you."

She smiled, but not for long. "Jake," she whispered. "I've been doing a lot of thinking since yesterday and—" She looked down. "I think it was a mistake. You and I not being only friends anymore."

"Aletta." He turned to face her. "You just need time, that's all. And I'll give it to you. As much time as you need."

She shook her head. "I can't . . . I can't, Jake. I'm sorry."

She turned to leave, but he took hold of her hands, and she didn't pull away. But he could feel the struggle inside her, could see the fear in her eyes. Fear that—instead of pushing him away—had the exact opposite effect.

"I love you, Aletta. And I'm fairly certain you love me. Though not as much as you will twenty years from now when I'm old and bald."

She gave a throaty laugh but shook her head again. "I can't go through that pain again, Jake. I'm not that strong."

"But you are that strong, Aletta. If it came to it, you would be. God would give you the strength," he whispered, his throat threatening to close. "And don't think I'm not a little scared too. Because I am." He gently wiped the tears from her cheeks. "But what scares me more than the thought of one day losing you . . . is the thought of not having spent my lifetime loving you."

She hiccupped a breath just as the kitchen door opened.

"Funniest thing, I got all the way to that spring house then plumb forgot what I'd—" Tempy stopped in her tracks and looked between the two of them. Then slowly looked up.

Jake followed her gaze, as did Aletta, and he saw a sprig of mistletoe hanging above them. He smiled, but Aletta only looked back at him, her expression saying she wasn't yet convinced. But that was all right. He had a little time yet. And though Aletta Prescott didn't know it, he could be awfully persuasive when he put his mind to it.

He leaned down and kissed her forehead, lingering only a second before he turned and walked out the door, tossing Tempy a discreet wink.

CHAPTER 18

On opening day of the auction, with dawn's first blush barely tracing the horizon, Aletta descended the stairs to the kitchen to the sounds of clanging pots and pans and the sweet aroma of Christmas simmering spices. The past week had flown by in a flurry of final details, and today at noon the auction would begin. She was even more excited—and nervous—than she'd anticipated.

She hoped the venture turned out to be profitable. Not only so she could prove Jake wrong, which would be enjoyable enough. But so that all the weeks of work from dozens and dozens of women would prove worthwhile.

She passed a window and caught a glimpse of someone entering the barn. Jake. Already up with the sun, working as hard as anyone, which spoke volumes about the man he was.

"You just need time, that's all," he'd told her. *"And I'll give it to you. As much time as you need."*

And he was giving her just that. And keeping his distance too. Somewhat. If she didn't count the occasional sprig of holly or out-of-season wildflower that just happened to appear in a little glass by the sink where she washed dishes. Or the pretty ear bobs that were waiting in a tiny decorative box by her bedroom door the other morning. Or the sketch of "General Prescott's Nativity" that hung, even now, on a board above one of the worktables.

But it wasn't time she needed so much as a guarantee. And as she already knew so well, life never came with one of those.

The heady aroma of coffee brewing on the stove greeted her as she rounded the corner and spotted Tempy cracking eggs into a bowl.

"No matter what time I rise, Tempy, you're already down here at work. Eggs gathered and sausage already brought up from the root cellar."

The older woman smiled. "I'm old and can't sleep no more like I used to. That's one of the things folks don't tell you when you're young, Missus Prescott. That one day your body's just gonna up and decide it don't need to rest like your mind tells it to."

Aletta smiled and reached for an iron skillet to fry up the sausage, the woman's comment spurring a question. "How long have you been here, Tempy? At Carnton, I mean."

"Oh, land sakes . . ." Tempy paused. "Nigh onto sixty-five years, I guess. I was all of maybe two or three when Master Randal, that be Mister McGavock's father, bought me and Mama from over in Montgomery."

Aletta looked over at her. Tempy stated it so matter-of-factly, about being bought and sold. And it occurred to Aletta then that she'd never had occasion to know a slave as well as she knew Tempy. A measure of shame accompanied that realization, as did a puzzlement. She chose her words carefully. "My understanding, Tempy, is that all the other slaves here at Carnton were sent south when the war started. And yet . . . you're still here."

"That's 'cuz I'm near ancient, Missus Prescott. Guess Mister and Missus McGavock figured the Federal Army wouldn't reckon an old woman like me was worth freein'." Tempy stilled and met Aletta's gaze, a knowing look moving into her eyes. "And I guess they was right," she finished succinctly, then dropped the remnants of a cracked eggshell into the compost bucket and turned back to her work.

But for Aletta, the air in the room seemed to evaporate.

From rote memory, she lit the stove, placed the skillet atop a burner, then sliced and pattied out the pork sausage, the image of a young black girl no more than two or three filling her mind. So many other questions she wanted to ask. But had no right to. What must it have been like to have

211

had all the choices in life taken from you? Your freedom stripped away?

As she placed the sausage in the skillet, the meat sizzling, aromas rising, Aletta realized with both a grateful and humble heart that at least she had choices. Choices that were hers alone to make.

A while later, after the McGavocks' breakfast was served, Aletta hurried back upstairs to rouse Andrew and get him dressed. In a blink, it would be noon and the auction would be under way. And there was still much to be done.

She returned to find the kitchen abuzz with hired help and volunteers. Voices and footfalls from the upstairs signaled that Mrs. McGavock was readying to give tours of the main floor of the home. Mrs. McGavock's mother, Mrs. Winder, along with a cousin, had arrived two days earlier with plans to stay through Christmas. Both women had jumped right in to help, including assisting with the decoration of the nine-foot cedar tree now standing statuesquely in the front hallway.

Tempy had Andrew's eggs waiting at the table in the corner for him, scrambled like he liked them, and he dove in, eating not one but two slices of warm pumpkin bread. Aletta didn't object when she spotted Tempy slipping him a fresh butter cookie. She was stepping in to see how she might best serve preparations in the kitchen when a voice interrupted her thoughts.

"Mrs. Prescott?"

Aletta turned to see Mrs. Buckner, one of the younger widows, standing in the doorway. She looked for the woman's precious twin girls but didn't see them.

"Mrs. Prescott, where would you like for us to put all the pies and cakes the women are bringing?"

Aletta gestured. "All the baked goods go to the barn. Mrs. Hunter and her group already have the tables set up and are pricing everything."

Mrs. Buckner nodded then hesitated before stepping forward. "Mrs. Prescott . . . me and the other ladies, we all want to thank you for all you've done to bring this event together."

The bustle of activity around them halted, and Aletta looked about the kitchen and met gaze after gaze.

"I was speaking with Mrs. McGavock a moment ago," Mrs. Buckner continued, "and she said you've worked almost night and day for weeks, and that the committee couldn't have done this without your leadership."

Aletta briefly bowed her head. "Mrs. McGavock is a very gracious woman."

"That may be, but . . . with the women coming together in recent days, getting to know each other, sharing our stories . . ." The young widow

213

smiled. "It's helped us all so much. It's helped me to know that I'm not alone. This time of year is supposed to be a joyous occasion . . . and it is," she added quickly. "But it can sometimes be so lonely too. So . . . thank you from all of us for making it far less so this year."

"You're most welcome," Aletta whispered. "Thanks to all of you as well. Because we've accomplished this together."

Everyone returned to their tasks, and she spotted Andrew hopping down from his chair.

"Are you finished, sweetheart?"

He nodded. "Mama . . . do you think Papa can hear us from where he is?"

Surprised at his question, she brushed the hair back from his forehead and prayed for wisdom, cherishing how much of Warren she saw in his expression. "I believe that—" She paused as a better, clearer response nudged hers from her mind. "—Jesus hears us and then passes our messages along to him."

His brow furrowed. "So . . . if there's somethin' I wanna tell Papa, I can just say it to Jesus?"

Aletta smiled. "Yes, sweetheart. You can say it to Jesus. Anything, anytime, anywhere, and he'll hear you. No matter if you whisper." She made her voice soft. "Or if you only say it in your heart. He hears everything. And he understands."

The edges of his little mouth nudged upward

and he hugged her tight. "I wanna go find Winder. But . . . can the two of us come back down later and maybe lick some of the cake bowls?"

She smiled. "Of course you can." She walked with him upstairs, wanting to see how plans were progressing outside the kitchen.

A length of red velvet rope had been draped across the staircase leading to the second-floor landing where the family bedrooms resided. And Mrs. Louisa McGavock, Mr. McGavock's sister-in-law who had graciously agreed to act as a docent for the tours, stood guard, her kind but firm smile at the ready.

Passing the front parlor, Aletta spotted Mrs. Felicia Grundy Porter, a relative of Mrs. McGavock and dedicated president of the Women's Relief Society. Mrs. Grundy had graciously agreed to direct a group of children in a tableau. But the woman already appeared slightly frazzled, her supposed-to-be silent and motionless costumed participants jabbering like little magpies.

Aletta fought back a smile and gave the woman an encouraging look.

Finally, she and Andrew discovered Winder, Hattie, and Miss Clouston on the front porch overseeing the bustle of activity outside, which was a sight to behold. And there, in the midst of it all, was Jake unloading donated items from wagon beds, along with crates of preserves and endless cakes, pies, and cookies. Not to mention the textiles—beautifully embroidered pillowcases and handkerchiefs, baby bibs, quilts of all sizes, and knitted throws. Some of which she'd helped with at the church building. These women truly had given their best.

Now if only people from Nashville and the neighboring communities would attend the auction and purchase items as hoped, so that the proceeds could benefit as many soldiers as possible, both those well and those wounded, like Emmett Zachary.

Last she'd spoken to Kate, Emmett's wounds were healing well. But the doctor had informed them that Emmett's wait for an artificial limb could be seven months or more. Kate had shared that the emotional strain of Emmett losing his leg, compounded by his lack of mobility, was wearing him—and his hope—thin.

"Captain Winston!" Andrew called, and Aletta looked back in time to see Andrew running full out, Winder right behind him.

Jake turned and spotted the boys and hopped down from the wagon bed in time to brace himself as they barreled into him. Miss Clouston and Hattie laughed beside her, and Aletta smiled, but her insides were a tangle of emotions.

Jake looked up at her in that moment, a boy dangling from each arm, and his smile softened, his expression filled with something far more than friendship. And he didn't seem the least bothered that someone else might see it. Even at this distance, Aletta could feel her attraction to him, the tug of his heart on hers.

Without warning, Andrew and Winder let go and grabbed Jake by his legs, nearly causing him to topple. With a deep growl, Jake grabbed them both, one under each arm, and spun the boys around until they screamed, "Uncle!"

"Mrs. Prescott?"

Aletta turned to see Mrs. McGavock standing just inside the entrance hall, the front door ajar, and joined her. "Good morning, Mrs. McGavock."

"Good morning, my dear. Isn't the weather lovely? So warm for December. And so promising for a strong attendance on this first day!"

"I couldn't agree more, ma'am."

"Firstly, I want to reiterate what Tempy said she's already told you. That you may take whatever time you need to rest. Delegate, Mrs. Prescott. And together we'll all rally and get the work done."

"Yes, ma'am. I'll do that."

Mrs. McGavock briefly covered Aletta's hands. "And if I haven't told you often enough in recent days . . . the promise of this event's success has been greatly increased by your tireless efforts. So I, along with the Women's Relief Society committee, salute you. In fact"— Mrs. McGavock gestured to a handsome and

217

well-dressed woman standing only feet away who joined them—"allow me to introduce my dear sister-in-law, Mrs. William Giles Harding of Belle Meade Plantation. Elizabeth is Mr. McGavock's sister—"

Aletta nodded.

"—and she's expressed a keen interest in thanking you personally for your work on the auction, Mrs. Prescott." Mrs. McGavock finished out the introductions.

"It's my pleasure to meet you, Mrs. Harding." Aletta dipped her head.

"Likewise, Mrs. Prescott. This auction promises to be the Women's Relief Society's most successful event to date, and I applaud your coordination. My sister-in-law, Carrie, here can only sing your praises, which I echo with full confidence."

Aletta felt her cheeks growing warm. "Thank you both, but it's been my honor to help. It's also been my saving grace," she added softly, glimpsing understanding in Mrs. McGavock's eyes.

After Mrs. Harding took her leave, Mrs. McGavock leaned close. "What you may not be aware of, Mrs. Prescott, is that my sister-in-law's husband, General William Giles Harding, is currently imprisoned in the North by the Federal Army. So truly, she's most grateful for our assisting the soldiers."

Aletta glanced back in Elizabeth Harding's direction. That woman's husband was in prison? Again she was reminded of how wrong it was—not to mention unwise—to make judgments based upon first impressions.

"One more thing I need to speak with you about, Mrs. Prescott." Mrs. McGavock leaned close. "It's something Winder and the Colonel mentioned to me this morning. I told them I'd need to secure your permission first before they said anything to Andrew. But I believe you know the boys are planning a *sleepout* in the spring."

Aletta nodded.

"Their thought was, especially in light of how fair the weather is, that they might do the sleepout this weekend, on Sunday night It'll be chilly, I'm certain. But not overly so, and they can bundle up, build a fire. The Colonel will be with them the entire time. But I sincerely doubt they'll want to stay out there the whole night."

"I think it's a wonderful idea, Mrs. McGavock. And I appreciate your sensitivity to my son's welfare. And to my own."

"I'm grateful God brought you to my door, Mrs. Prescott. I only wish we could continue your employment after the New Year. But I'm already praying for God to guide your next steps in that regard."

Aletta managed a smile, what hope she'd had of possibly staying on here meeting a swift and decisive end. "Thank you, Mrs. McGavock."

"Oh gracious . . ." Mrs. McGavock glanced at the clock on a nearby table. "It's time to meet with the committee, and I've forgotten my notes. I'd best run upstairs and get them."

"Let me do that for you, ma'am."

"Oh no, I couldn't ask you to—"

"I'm fine, Mrs. McGavock." Aletta gave a smile. "I'll bring your notes right back down. Where are they?"

"Bless you, dear. They're in my bedroom. On my bedside table. Thank you, Mrs. Prescott."

Upon Mrs. Louisa McGavock's official lowering of the rope, Aletta climbed the stairs to the second floor landing, a bit winded but fine.

She'd been to the schoolroom several times but never into the McGavocks' bedroom. She opened the door and quickly found Mrs. McGavock's notes. She turned to go when a portrait in an oval frame over the fireplace, of three girls, caught her attention. One of them resembled Hattie so much—the girl's cute little button nose—that Aletta knew it must be her.

But the two others . . .

Two perfectly beautiful children, one brunette, the other blond, cheeks rosy, expressions so serene and happy. And both, she assumed with certainty, gone now. Carrie McGavock was, indeed, well acquainted with grief. Odd how the knowledge of another's suffering helped at times like this, and Aletta drew strength from it as she hurried back downstairs to help get the auction officially under way.

She assisted the women in the barn as they finished pricing and arranging the baked goods. Then she checked with the older children who were hosting the hot apple cider cart, the smell of spiced apples and cloves, roasting pork, and popped corn setting the perfect festive mood.

She caught sight of Jake looking at her from across the way and saw him pointing. She turned and looked in that direction—

And even after all the preparation and all the work, she found herself unprepared for the lines of wagons and throngs of people coming up the drive.

The next afternoon, Aletta sought solace from the crowds—the auction attendance higher today than the one previous—and she was grateful to find the kitchen empty and quiet. For the moment, at least. She checked her list for the next item to bake.

Pecan pies. Her favorite.

There was something special about the sugar-coated pecans and the gooey goodness of the filling that tasted like comfort. And home. She gathered the ingredients for the piecrusts and began working them together for the pastry as her thoughts wandered, questions never far from her mind moving closer. Come January, where would she and Andrew go? Where would they live?

Since room and board were included with this position, she'd managed to save almost all of her earnings. But Andrew . . . He was going to be heartbroken to leave Winder. And to think that the boys could continue to be playmates simply wasn't sensible.

She divided the pastry and began working the rolling pin over the first pie shell, pressing down harder than she'd intended. So she folded the dough over itself and started again.

And what of Jake? After the auction he would go back to the war, which only confirmed within her again that she'd made the right choice. No matter that her feelings sometimes challenged that decision.

"Rest assured, Captain"—Mrs. McGavock's voice drifted down the staircase leading to the kitchen—"we're so grateful you came when you did. It's been a pleasure having you here with us."

"It's been *my* pleasure, Mrs. McGavock. And I appreciate your understanding about my request to return to my regiment."

Aletta paused, rolling pin in hand. He was leaving? Already?

"Oh, I understand completely, Captain Winston. So does the Colonel. He and I both applaud your honor and dedication. In fact—"

Aletta felt guilty for listening to their conversation, but if they'd intended for it to be private, they should've chosen a more private setting. Still, she clanged a couple of pans together to soothe her conscience.

"Only last night," Mrs. McGavock continued, "the Colonel commented about how much he appreciates the work you've done not only on the auction but on the cabin, the barn, the smokehouse. He's been quite impressed with your handiwork and initiative."

"Again, ma'am, it's been my pleasure. I'm only sorry if when—"

The kitchen door opened and several volunteers entered, chatting and laughing, bringing the cool air in with them, and Aletta could no longer hear the conversation. And by the time things quieted down again, it was apparently over. She stared down at the piecrust.

So Jake was returning to his regiment. And at his own request, it seemed.

She reached for a bowl and cracked three eggs into it, then set butter to browning in a pan on the stove. That was good, that he was returning to his post. It was what she'd wanted. And what was best. He was well enough, after all. And she'd long held the opinion that every able-bodied man should be fighting. But . . .

The thought that something could happen to him formed a knot at the base of her throat. She measured a cup of sugar into the bowl and stirred. Andrew would be disappointed to learn of Jake's departure. But perhaps not as much as he would be when the time came for him to leave Winder, and Carnton, behind.

She reached for a dash of salt when movement outside the window drew her attention. Jake climbed up into a wagon and both boys scrambled up beside him. Andrew looked up at him and said something, and Jake nodded, then handed her son one of the reins. A dull ache filled her chest and began working its way up.

Still . . . it was a good thing Jake was leaving. A very good thing.

CHAPTER 19

"Who told you I was leaving?" Flat on his back beneath a wagon, Jake studied the broken axle, then finally peered up. But he couldn't decipher her expression.

"Well, I—" Aletta shrugged. "I happened to overhear a portion of your conversation with Mrs. McGavock yesterday afternoon. But in my defense," she said quickly, "I did clang some pots together to announce that someone was in the kitchen."

"Huh . . . And here I thought some actual cooking was going on."

She frowned. "So you're not leaving."

He crawled out from beneath the wagon, brushed the dirt from his clothes, and looked down at her. "No, Aletta. I'm not leaving. Not yet, anyway."

"But you said you'd requested a return to your regiment."

"That's right, I did."

"And yet you didn't say anything to me about it."

"Nope. I didn't." He grabbed a mallet, crawled

back beneath the wagon, and gave the busted axle a hard *thwack*. Not that it needed it, but it made him feel better.

Her disappointment that he'd be staying at Carnton a while longer confirmed that he'd made the right decision to request a return to service. Only, he wished now more than ever that Colonel Stratton had granted his approval. Instead of telling him to stay the course and get the sketches and the piece written for the newspaper as requested.

"But your superior officer said no?"

"That's right. So I'm here until the Colonel sends word otherwise."

"But why? Your shoulder is clearly healed. You're able to fight."

He peered up at her from beneath the wagon. "I'm glad you think so, Aletta. And if I thought it would change anything, I'd have you write my superior and share your opinion."

He tried to focus on the axle. And couldn't. How could she think so little of him—think that he'd stay out of the fight for such a petty reason? Clearly she didn't think as highly of him as he'd reckoned. He'd hoped she might have softened at least a little in regard to her feelings for him. But it seemed as though she'd made up her mind.

Requiring tools he didn't have at hand, he crawled out from beneath the wagon again.

"Is there something else you need, Aletta? If

not, I'd appreciate you leaving me to tend the wagon."

She suddenly seemed hesitant to meet his gaze. "Only that . . . Mrs. McGavock said she needs to speak with you when you have a moment. I don't know about what."

"I'll go see her shortly. As soon as I'm finished here." He strode to the back of the wagon, grabbed a cloth from a bucket, and wiped the grease from his hands.

It stung to discover she was so eager to see the back of him. He also didn't relish her learning the real reason he'd been sent here to recuperate. But if this was how things were going to be between them, he wouldn't have to tell her after all.

"You really are gifted at sketching, Jake."

He turned back to see her looking at his sketchbook that lay open on the workbench.

"May I?" she asked.

He shrugged.

She turned the pages slowly, sometimes smiling, other times just staring for a moment. Until she came to a picture of Andrew.

"Oh, Jake . . . This is beautiful. It looks just like him." She ran her forefinger over the sketch. "He looks happy. But also . . . sad. When did you draw this?"

"Last week. After he asked me if I missed my family."

Her gaze softened and she opened her mouth as

though to say something, then apparently thought better of it. She reached to turn the page and Jake almost stopped her, knowing which sketches were next.

She went absolutely still.

He watched her, the way she bit her lower lip, the sharp rise and fall of her chest, her emotions clearly warring inside her with a vengeance.

"The artist has been kind to me," she said softly, not looking at him.

"The artist drew what he saw. What he sees even now," he said.

A single tear slipped down her cheek. "I wish this were easier, Jake."

"Nothing is easy, Aletta. At least nothing worth having."

She turned to him and, for an instant, he saw the love in her eyes, her desire for him written so clearly in her expression. Then in a blink, those feelings were shuttered again, buried beneath the fear and the pain. And she walked away.

The next morning, Jake situated himself inside the door of the barn, ready to help where needed, but enjoying the opportunity to watch the flood of auction attendees as they wandered and pondered, shopped and bartered, ate and drank.

Pen and sketchbook at the ready, he could scarcely keep up with the images begging to be captured. That of Hattie and Andrew playing

Mary and Joseph again, and Andrew's absolute insistence that he get to hold the baby Jesus an equal amount of time, so he could "talk" to him, the boy said.

The giddiness on a little girl's face as she nibbled on a cookie while being chased by a newborn kitten. An old woman, her brow plowed with furrows of old age, holding a music box up to her ear, a tear trailing her check as the box plinked out a tune he didn't recognize. But that she obviously did.

Jake turned to a fresh page just as the embodiment of beauty walked into his line of sight. She was a good distance away, so her features weren't clear to him in the moment, but he knew them by heart. And his pencil took on a life of its own as he captured the curves of her mouth, the soft hollows of her cheeks, her eyes, her hair, the slender lines of her neck. And the distinctly feminine fullness of her body that nestled the heartbeat of a life within. They all poured from him in perfect, beautiful clarity.

An amputee caught his attention next, in a wheelchair, the man clearly uncomfortable with people watching him. But it was the way the former soldier watched them from where he sat off to the side, the yearning in his expression, his desire to walk so tangible that Jake felt the ache of it in his chest and rushed to capture the image. Then he saw Mrs. Zachary approach the man, and he realized who the amputee was. Jake stowed the notebook and pencil in a drawer of the workbench and went to meet them.

"Corporal Zachary." Jake offered his hand, not surprised that Zachary saluted him first before accepting.

"It's good to see you again, Captain Winston."

"You too, Corporal. Though I'm not sure I would've recognized you without your wife here. Last time I saw you, you were all bandaged up."

Zachary ran a hand over his stubbled jawline, the cuts and bruises still healing. "Doc finally took off the bandages this week. Which I told him might not be a good thing. Now my wife knows just how ugly I really am after all this."

They all laughed, but Jake caught the way Kate Zachary gently touched her husband's shoulder, as well as the fleeting shadow that eclipsed the Corporal's face. Zachary absently reached down and fiddled with the knot tied at the knee of his right pant leg.

"Kate?"

Jake turned to see Aletta approaching them in the crowd. She hugged Kate first, then greeted Zachary with a smile.

Kate squeezed her hand. "Aletta, you're looking radiant."

Aletta made a face. "I certainly don't feel that way, but you're kind to say so."

"Tell me," Kate continued. "How are you feeling?"

As the women stepped to one side to talk, Jake saw an opportunity. "Corporal, how about some hot apple cider? And maybe a slice of pork roast?"

"Sounds good to me, sir."

Zachary reached to push the wheels of his chair, but Jake beat him to it.

"I don't mind driving, Corporal, if you don't mind riding."

"I don't mind, Captain. Thank you, sir."

Jake steered the wheelchair over the rough terrain and closer to the fire pit where a roasted pig hung on a spit. With one of the ladies helping them, they had plates and cups in no time, and Jake enjoyed talking to a fellow soldier about the war, about where they'd fought, their various encampments, and the latest news. What little there was with the recent lull in fighting.

"So . . ." Jake laid aside his empty plate. "How are you doing, Zachary?"

The man didn't answer at first, then shook his head. "Not too good, Captain."

"Call me Jake. We're two soldiers at a Women's Relief Society event. I think we can stand a little informality."

Zachary laughed, then began to talk. About details obviously difficult for him to speak about, based on the ebb and flow of his words. And details also difficult to hear. But Jake wanted to listen, wanted to help. And by the time Aletta and Kate found them, he felt the flicker of an idea taking hold inside him.

An idea that hadn't come from him. But that was meant for him, he was certain. Now . . . what to do with it? That was the question.

"You could come on the sleepout with us too, Mama. If you want."

Aletta helped Andrew put on his coat, then buttoned it up. "I don't think Colonel McGavock would appreciate having me along. I think this is intended to be only for boys. Of all ages," she added, giving him a quick hug from behind.

What she didn't tell him was that she was eager to spend an hour soaking in a warm tub Tempy had offered to heat for her. Every muscle in her body ached from the long weekend of baking and cooking—Sunday's attendance equal or more to what it had been on Thursday, Friday, and Saturday—and she couldn't wait to sink down into that hot, sudsy water. And to wash her hair would be sheer heaven.

"Do you have your binoculars so you can see the stars up close?"

Andrew whipped out one of two pairs of paper binoculars that he and Winder had made in class with Miss Clouston, then eyed her. "Mama, these don't really make the stars bigger. They just—"

232

He thought for a moment. "—focus my attention on whatever I'm lookin' at."

"Ah . . ." She smiled. How she wished Warren were still here to see this, to watch their son growing up, to teach Andrew all he needed to know about being a man, lessons she couldn't begin to teach him.

But would have to. Somehow.

"What about your gloves, sweetheart?"

He pulled them from his pockets.

"And your scarf?"

"I'm not cold. I don't need it."

"But you *will* need it later when you get cold."

"I'm not gonna get cold. I'm already gettin' hot."

She grabbed the scarf and hurried him on downstairs to the entrance hall where the table clock was chiming the nine o'clock hour. And just as they heard Winder and Colonel McGavock's footsteps on the staircase, a knock sounded at the door.

Aletta answered. "Jake. Good evening."

He smiled and stepped inside. "Evening, Aletta. Are my campers ready?"

"Your campers?"

He eyed her. "Did . . . no one tell you?"

"Tell me wh—"

"Oh, my dear Mrs. Prescott—"

Aletta turned to Mrs. McGavock and Winder descending the stairs.

"It's my fault. I forgot to say anything to you about it. The Colonel was called to a meeting in town this afternoon and won't be back until quite late tonight. He didn't wish to cancel on the boys' special outing, so he asked Captain Winston to stand in for him."

"Oh . . ." Aletta nodded. "That's very kind of you, Captain Winston."

"Isn't it though?" Mrs. McGavock nodded. "Well, you three boys have fun now. And when you get too cold later on tonight, the front door will be unlocked, so come on inside."

"Get too cold?" Jake made a face that drew a giggle from the boys. "We men will be having too much fun to get cold."

"Yeah, Mama." Winder grinned. "We men'll be havin' fun!"

Andrew parroted the same, his face bright with anticipation.

"Andrew, be sure and keep your coat on, honey. You don't want to get sick."

But Aletta knew he didn't hear her. He was too busy talking.

The threesome left by way of the front door, and Mrs. McGavock closed it behind them with a sigh. "They'll have a marvelous time together and will come back with tales they'll regale us with for a week. Meanwhile, you get some much-needed rest, Mrs. Prescott. Enjoy this rare time alone."

"Oh yes, I will, Mrs. McGavock. Thank you."

Aletta bid her good night and started back toward the kitchen through the study, then paused and waited to hear the retreat of Mrs. McGavock's footsteps on the stairs before making a beeline out the front door.

CHAPTER 20

"Jake!" Aletta hurried after them, the muscles in her abdomen complaining.

Jake paused and looked back, the boys beside him.

Winded when she reached them, her side aching, Aletta paused for a few seconds to catch her breath. "I just needed to tell you that—" She swallowed. "Sometimes . . . Andrew has a tendency . . . to not wear his coat."

"Mama, I'm not cold."

Aletta held up a forefinger. "But you will be if you take off your coat. And then you'll get a cold."

"That's what my mama says too, Mrs. Prescott. But I never do get sick. I always—" Winder stopped. His face crinkled up and he sneezed, which made Andrew laugh, which then started a fake sneezing contest between them.

"Please, Jake." Aletta lowered her voice. "Make sure he keeps it on. He was born prematurely and has always had a tendency toward illness. So it's important that he stays warm."

"I'll take good care of him, Aletta. Don't you worry."

She nodded. "Are you going far?"

"Not too far. I scouted out a place just across that field and over the ridge."

He pointed, and she peered in that direction as though she could see anything besides darkness, and maybe the faintest outline of the trees.

"Aletta," he said softly.

She looked back.

"He'll be fine. I'll bring him back to you first thing in the morning unharmed and still in one piece."

Again she nodded, then pulled Andrew to her and gave him a hug and kiss.

"Mom!" He pulled away. "Not on a sleepout!"

"My mama does that too," Winder said as they walked away, and Aletta could still hear his and Andrew's exchange as they started across the field.

The night was cold without her coat, and she hurried back inside and stood in the entrance hall for a moment, her imagination running wild with all that could go wrong, with all the ways Andrew could get hurt.

She'd recently read about some Federal troops who'd taken to raiding local farms, stealing whatever they could. What if that group of soldiers happened upon Jake and the boys tonight? What would they—

"Please, Lord, keep them safe," she whispered aloud, working to silence her worry that she knew was unfounded. She knew at heart that her heightened concern had more to do with Warren's passing than with Andrew. Yet if anything happened to him too . . .

Telling herself he would be fine, she returned to the kitchen and found Tempy pouring the last kettle of heated water into the bathtub that was situated in front of the hearth, the fire crackling with warmth. She got teary-eyed just looking at it.

"I done pulled the curtains closed, ma'am. And with all the menfolk outta the house, it's just us. So you go on and get undressed, and I'll help you in. Don't want you fallin' on Tempy time."

Aletta had to smile. She did as asked, feeling a little self-conscious about her body as she undressed, the air cold. But as soon as she stepped into the tub and sank down into the water, she felt herself relaxing.

"It's important not to get the water too hot for a woman in your state, ma'am. But I can add a little more as we go along if you need it."

Aletta sighed, able to feel the soreness in her body melting away. "It's wonderful, Tempy. Thank you." Then she started to cry. And couldn't stop. "I'm-I'm sorry," she finally managed, trying to hold herself together.

"Ain't no reason to say you're sorry. Not to me, anyway. You just let the tears come, ma'am. You got every reason under heaven to be cryin'. And just 'cuz you cryin' don't mean you don't trust the good Lawd no more either. Jesus knows that. Shoot, even he cried when he was here. Over that good ol' friend of his who died 'fore the Lawd could get there to save him. And what with Jesus already knowin' he was 'bout to give Lazarus back his life. Makes me wanna cry just thinkin' about it."

Aletta looked back and, sure enough, tears filled Tempy's eyes. Then Tempy grinned, and Aletta felt a bubble of laughter work its way up her throat. She sank deeper into the tub, relishing the moment.

"Want me to wash your hair for you, ma'am? I do Mrs. McGavock's."

"If you don't mind, Tempy."

The woman made a tsking noise. "If I don't mind . . ." She laughed. "You done brought so much joy to my kitchen, I'm happy to do it for you."

Aletta loosened the pins from her hair then dunked several times until it was thoroughly wet. Tempy lathered up the soap and began working it through, and Aletta closed her eyes, certain she'd slipped through the veil and into heaven.

A while later, hair in a towel and skin pruning, she climbed from the tub with Tempy's help and dried off, shivering as Tempy helped her into her nightgown.

"You carryin' that baby awful high, ma'am. And you know what that means."

Aletta ran her hands over her belly. "Boy or girl, it doesn't matter to me. I just pray he or she is healthy."

"Mmm-hmm. I hear that, ma'am. Now sit down here in this chair by the fire and let me brush that hair 'til it's dry."

An hour or so later, her hair all but dry and more relaxed than she could remember, Aletta rose. "I can't thank you enough for this, Tempy. And . . . for welcoming me as you have into your kitchen."

Tempy searched her expression then gave her arm a gentle squeeze. "You gonna be all right, ma'am. Even if it don't feel that way from time to time. I 'member when my husband, Isum, died. Big old mountain of a man, he was. I come in one evenin', found him crumpled right there on the floor of the cabin out back. Already gone. Felt like someone ripped my heart out and stomped on it. Still does, some days, when I go missin' him. Most days, though, I think of him waitin' for me yonder on them golden streets, and that gives my heart a joy my chest can barely hold." Her smile said what words never could. "The Lord'll give you what you need when you need it, Missus Prescott. He always does. You just need to keep watchin' for it so's you don't miss it."

Still sifting Tempy's counsel, Aletta climbed the stairs to her room. She looked out the window toward the field where she'd last seen Jake and the boys, said a prayer for them all, and was asleep within seconds of her head touching the pillow.

"You put the blade of grass between your thumbs, like this." Jake showed the boys by the flicker of the campfire. "A thicker blade of grass works best. Then you cup your hands together and blow like this." He blew through his thumbs, and the boys' eyes lit.

"I wanna do it!" Winder scooted closer.

"Me too!"

Jake took turns showing them how, then they settled onto their pallets for some hot chocolate and butter cookies, compliments of Tempy. He figured it was a bit past two o'clock, maybe a little later, and he couldn't believe they were both still awake. So far they'd done plenty of stargazing, he'd told them stories he remembered from childhood, and they'd asked him about what he did in the army—which he'd kept to generalities. They'd told him every joke they'd ever heard, it seemed like, and had even started making some up.

The way they bantered back and forth and got to laughing over nothing and everything reminded him of how he and Freddie used to carry on as boys.

Jake looked over to find them both asleep. But he knew that if he didn't keep the promise he'd made to them earlier, he'd pay for it dearly. So no going to sleep for him. He added more wood to the fire, then sat back and enjoyed the sound of the wind through the winter grasses and studied the night sky for a while, the stars a distant blur against a wash of black.

Sometime later, he retrieved his notebook and spectacles and began sketching. He already had the drawings he needed for the newspaper article. Problem would be choosing which ones to include and what to say about the auction overall. As the night sky deepened, he knew the first blush of dawn wasn't long away, which meant that he needed to—

Then he heard it. Somewhere behind him. A rustling in the grass.

That much noise was no small animal, and he pulled his rifle closer. Whatever it was, was still some distance away, just over the ridge. Not about to leave the boys, he took off his spectacles and moved just beyond the circle of firelight and into the darkness. His eyes quickly adjusted, and then he saw her. Or was fairly certain it was her. What other woman would be out here walking the field this time of the morning?

"Aletta?"

"Good morning, Jake," she whispered, the *swoosh* of her skirts enough to wake every animal between there and Kentucky. *This woman . . .*

"What are you doing out here?" As if he didn't already know.

She held up a basket as she came closer. "I brought some pie and milk. And some coffee. I thought you all might be hungry. How are the boys doing?"

He took the basket from her and caught a whiff of lilac and something else sweet and womanly. "They're sleeping for now. But the sun will be coming up soon, so I need to wake them shortly for one last bit of stargazing."

She knelt by Andrew and tucked his blanket closer about him, then did the same to Winder. Neither boy stirred.

"Well . . ." She rose. "I guess I should head on back to the house."

"Thank you for the pie and drinks. We'll enjoy them."

She turned to go then paused. "Would you mind terribly if I stayed for a while? I promise I won't get in the way."

Open to her company anytime, anywhere, Jake gestured to his pallet and claimed a space opposite the fire from her.

"So what's it been like?" she asked after a moment. "The *sleepout*."

He gave her a quick summary of what they'd

done and talked about, and as he watched her watching her son sleep, he got an inkling of how difficult it must have been for her to watch them walk away last night. The boy was her world now. Him, along with the child she was carrying. They were all she had left of her husband. So he didn't blame her for being a bit overprotective.

The silence lengthened and the crackle of the flames filled the quiet between them.

"Thank you for your kindness to Emmett Zachary, Jake. It meant a lot to Kate. And to me too."

"I was happy to do it." Tempted to tell her about the idea he'd been turning around in his head, he decided it was a mite soon. Besides, it might scare her off, and he was working hard on being patient.

She pulled his blanket up over her. "Mrs. McGavock told me this afternoon that the auction has already brought in almost as much money as they'd estimated for the entire event. And we still have another four days."

"It's been a great success, Aletta. You should be proud."

"I am. And I'm also grateful to you for all your help."

"I just did what you told me to do."

She laughed. "I know. That's what I'm grateful for."

He smiled, sensing a layer or two of her

244

wall coming down. He enjoyed the chance to watch her as she told him about things that had happened behind the scenes over the past few days. Finally, a comfortable silence settled between them and they stared up at the stars.

"Captain Winston?" Andrew stirred beside him and yawned. "Is it time yet?"

"Almost, buddy. I was just about to wake you. Someone I think you may know has joined us." Jake hoped the boy wouldn't resent his mother being here.

Andrew looked over his shoulder. "Mama," he whispered, and smiled. "We've been havin' fun."

"That's what I hear."

Andrew sat up. "Captain, can I look through your rifle glass again?"

Jake smiled and handed it to him. "Rifle sight."

"Rifle sight," the boy repeated "Captain Winston is a sharpshooter, Mama. That means he can shoot just about anything, no matter how far away it is."

"Is that right?" she said softly, and Jake heard a touch of uncertainty in her voice, as though she were questioning if he'd told the boys more than she might approve of.

Andrew held the sight to his eye and looked up, then finally exhaled. "I can't get it to work anymore." The boy handed it to him. "Can you fix it?"

Jake pointed. "Remember to turn that little

knob to the left or right until what you're looking at becomes clear."

Andrew tried again. "It's still not workin'.""

Jake took it from him, went through the motions of holding it up to his eye and squinting, then turned the knob a little and handed it back, aware of Aletta watching him.

The boy shook his head. "I think it's broken."

"Here . . ." Aletta reached for it. "Let me try."

She peered through the sight and adjusted the lens, then handed it back to him. "There you go. All fixed."

Andrew lay back down and stared up while Jake busied himself with tending the fire.

"I can't find the Big Dipper anymore, Captain Winston."

Jake glanced up, the night sky a blur, and he grew a little uncomfortable. "Sure you can. It's right up there."

"Right up where?"

Jake felt the back of his neck heat. "Why don't we wake up Winder, give him a chance to find it."

He coaxed Winder awake, and the boy searched the night sky, but he couldn't locate the constellation either. The boys sat there looking at him, and if Jake hadn't known better, he would've thought he was being set up. But he did know better. No one here knew about that injury. But this wasn't the time or place to—

"The Big Dipper is just over the height of that tallest tree right there." Aletta leaned forward, pointing. "And once you see that, you should be able to see the bear."

"I see it!" Winder grinned, then handed Andrew the sight, and he took a turn. Then the boy passed it to Jake, and Jake again went through the motions, looking in the same direction they had.

Aletta reached for the basket. "How about some pecan pie and milk?"

She served them each a slice, and they ate in silence as the sun came up, the boys nearly nodding off again, while Jake quietly savored the taste of home—the sweet and buttery filling with pecans on top crusted in syrup. How he'd missed this.

"This is just like my own mama used to make," he said after a moment. "Thank you."

"You're welcome," she whispered, then began gathering everything back into the basket.

He did likewise with the camp and when they reached the house, he dropped the boys' pallets inside the front hallway and turned to leave.

"Jake . . ."

He paused, and the look in her eyes unnerved him.

"Thank you again for accompanying the boys on their sleepout. I can tell they really enjoyed it."

"You're welcome. I enjoyed it too."

She opened her mouth as if about to say something else, then merely smiled and closed the door. And that's when he was all but certain she knew the truth. Or at the very least, she suspected it.

CHAPTER 21

Why hadn't he told her the truth?

The question kept turning over and over in Aletta's mind as she worked beside Tempy preparing breakfast for the McGavock family that morning, then as the hired cooks and volunteers arrived and yet another day of baking and cooking for the auction got under way.

Yet deep down she knew why. But what bothered her far more was her own audacity in repeatedly questioning his motives in being here. Not only to herself, but to him. She had even questioned whether he'd really been wounded or not.

A sharpshooter who could no longer see well enough to shoot. Or at least, not at a distance.

"Mrs. Prescott, we need more flour and sugar, ma'am. And eggs. Mrs. Prescott?"

Aletta looked up, the request slowly registering. "Yes, of course. I'll be right back." She retrieved the keys to the larder and fetched the needed supplies for the other cooks.

She had to see him, apologize to him. He'd repeatedly offered her kindness and friendship, and she'd held him suspect from the very start. Then he'd offered her far more, and she'd turned that down too. A decision she'd begun to question more and more.

She slid the first four pans of shortbread into the oven, then hurried upstairs to check on Andrew. Still fast asleep. The boy would likely sleep until noon, if not later.

Downstairs, she grabbed her shawl from the hook in the kitchen. "Tempy, I'll be back in a few minutes. I need to go do something."

"No problem, ma'am. We're doin' fine here. Runnin' a little ahead of the clock even."

Aletta opened the kitchen door then paused, seeing a cardinal perched on a tree branch just a few feet from where she stood. The brilliantly colored bird didn't spook, didn't fly away. He just sat there, looking at her. Then he sang.

The most beautiful little warble, his chest puffing out as though he knew how strikingly handsome he was, and how rare. She heard soft footsteps behind her.

"Would you look at that, Missus Prescott." Tempy's voice held a smile. "A red bird in winter. When you see a red bird in winter, you'll prosper in spring. But when you hear a red bird sing—"

"Your sadness will soon be lifted," Aletta said softly, knowing the old wives' tale. As she made her way to the cabin, she only hoped that would hold true.

Jake pushed from bed and ran a hand through his hair, having managed to get a couple hours of sleep. Yet knowing his assistance would be needed for the auction that day, he fed the fire in the hearth and stoked it back to life, then filled the cast iron kettle with water and hung it over the flame. Coffee was his first order of business.

That, and going to see Aletta.

Exhausted as he'd been, he'd still lain awake thinking about her, thinking about the way she'd looked at him. Might as well go ahead and face the truth straight up and get it over with.

The water in the kettle had just reached a boil when a knock sounded on the door. He glanced around for his pants, found them on the chair, and pulled them on over his long johns.

He opened the door. "Aletta."

"I need to apologize to you, Jake. And I'd be obliged if you'd allow me to do that."

He stared, a little baffled, then nodded. "All right."

"I'm sorry for questioning whether or not you were truly wounded."

He looked away.

"For questioning why you were here instead of being off fighting somewhere. This auction, all the money being raised, all the good being done, is due in large part to you. I appreciate your friendship to me. And also your friendship with my son."

He slowly looked back.

"And I only hope," she continued, her smile reaching her eyes before it turned the beautiful curves of her mouth, "that I haven't overstepped my bounds in a way that will prevent that friendship from continuing in the future."

Hearing the ring of familiarity of his words in hers, he smiled. And dared to hope.

"Not at all. Our friendship can sustain that, and a whole lot more, I assure you."

A light came into her eyes that he felt deep inside his chest.

CHAPTER 22

CHRISTMAS DAY
DECEMBER 25, 1863

Aletta dressed hurriedly, scarcely able to wait for Andrew to get downstairs and find his gift waiting beneath the tree. But the boy was still fast asleep. She'd ordered his gift from a mercantile in Nashville and had feared it wouldn't arrive in time, but it had. She only hoped it would meet with his expectations. Especially this Christmas.

She paused and looked at him, his little chest rising and falling with easy slumber. Recalling how the auction had drawn to a close yesterday in a grand celebration with a bonfire and Christmas carols, and special sweets for the children, she knew he'd sleep for a while yet.

How had the two of them come to be among such fine, good people whom—up until only a handful of weeks ago—she'd never even met? Same for so many of the women she'd gotten to know through the Women's Relief Society— women she shared so much in common with.

How often she'd questioned God's goodness and doubted his provision. But in this moment, she could see it. God's hand. And even though she didn't know what the future held, she knew who held it.

And somehow, she could even feel Warren's love in a way she hadn't in a very long time. As if responding to her thoughts, their child within her moved.

Patience, little one . . . I'll tell you all about him as you grow up.

She heard movement in the kitchen and knew Tempy was already awake. But when she rounded the corner and saw who was seated at the breakfast table, coffee cup in hand, she realized she'd been mistaken. Happily so.

"Merry Christmas, Jake. You're up early."

He smiled. "Merry Christmas. Is he up yet?"

She shook her head. "Still sawing logs. Are you hungry?"

"Always. Want me to do the eggs?"

She passed him a bowl in response, and he went straight to work.

"Well, Merry Christmas to me," Tempy said a few minutes later when she walked in to find the breakfast ready and waiting.

Aletta hugged her tight. "Merry Christmas, Tempy."

"Merry Christmas, Missus Prescott. I just checked on him, and he's still sleepin'."

Aletta poured the coffee. "Thank you both for being so excited about this with me. I think he's going to love it!"

Jake just winked.

Together with Miss Clouston who joined them, they enjoyed eggs, bacon, and Aletta's angel biscuits. Then Aletta and Tempy started on the family's Christmas brunch while Miss Clouston and Jake went on upstairs.

No sooner did Aletta hear the patter of Andrew's footsteps on the staircase behind her than she heard the thunder of Winder's coming down the front stairs.

"Andrew!" Winder yelled. "You got something under the tree!"

Andrew let out a whoop and both boys shot up the stairs, headed for the entrance hall.

"Wait for us!" Aletta called, tossing her apron aside.

To her relief, Jake was guarding the tree—one boy under each arm. And Miss Clouston was opening the curtains.

Hattie flew down the stairs, followed by the Colonel and Mrs. McGavock, already dressed. Same for Mrs. Winder and Mrs. McGavock's cousin, Miss Templeton, who were still with them. They all exchanged greetings, then each of the children burrowed beneath the tree to find their present.

Andrew pulled out a box wrapped in blue

paper. "This one has my name on it, Mama!"

"So it does." Aletta smiled, watching Andrew stare at the box for the longest time even as Winder and Hattie had already opened their gifts.

"Santa brought me a doll!" Hattie held up a beautiful porcelain-faced doll then hugged her tight.

"Look what he brought me!" Beaming, Winder help up a box full of painted toy soldiers all standing at attention, perfectly in a row.

Aletta looked back at Andrew. "Aren't you going to open yours?"

Andrew nodded, then tore into the package, and Aletta could hardly wait to see his reaction.

He held up the box, a smile on his face. But it wasn't the smile she'd expected.

"It's a train," he said. "A blue one."

Aletta knelt beside him. "I know it's not the color you wanted, but it's got cars that attach and the locomotive even has a bell that rings."

He nodded. "I like it!" But she could see that it wasn't what he'd wanted, and her heart fell.

Miss Clouston distributed the rest of the gifts beneath the tree, then paused. "Andrew . . ." She glanced at Aletta, a question in her gaze. "You have another gift, dear. But it's in the tree. And this one . . . isn't wrapped."

Andrew put down his train and walked over. He looked at where Miss Clouston pointed and his face lit. "My train! *This* is the train Papa promised me!" He pulled a little red engine from the branches of the tree. "And it's red. Just like I wanted!"

Confused, Aletta joined him, and Andrew held up the toy, a tag bearing his name hanging off the smokestack. "All really good trains are red, Mama," he said, as though everyone should know that.

The train was hand carved, not nearly as detailed as the one she'd ordered from the Nashville mercantile, and it had no railcars and certainly didn't make any sounds. But when she turned the train over and saw the writing on the bottom, she felt the prick of tears. *I love you, buddy, Jake.*

She read the inscription aloud, and Andrew's eyes lit. He raced over to Jake, who knelt and hugged him tight.

"I love my train!" Andrew drew back. "Does this mean I get to call you Jake now?"

Jake looked across the room at her, much like everyone else, and Aletta smiled. "I imagine that would be just fine."

Andrew gave a loud shout and went to show Winder his red engine. Aletta joined Jake, who stood quietly off to the side.

"How did you know?" She searched his gaze. "That was the kind of train he wanted? And that he wanted red?"

"I didn't. But that's the kind of train I had when

I was his age. Besides . . . aren't all really good trains red?"

"Mama, it's snowing!" Andrew called, racing back into the entrance hall.

Sure enough, Aletta looked outside and saw big, fat flakes of snow drifting down. Watching the children peer out the window, she turned beside her. "Thank you, Jake. For everything."

"My pleasure, Aletta. And I have something special to share with you later today too. It's a Christmas gift, of sorts. But we'll need to ride into town to see it."

"Into town?" She eyed him. "Well then, Tempy and I best get back downstairs and finish getting brunch—" Her breath caught. She grabbed Jake's arm for support. "Oh . . ." She grimaced, a sharp pain arcing over her belly.

"Aletta!" His arm came around her waist.

"Oh, Missus Prescott." Tempy came alongside her. "Are you all right?"

Aletta's breath came in short, sharp gasps.

"Mrs. McGavock!" Jake called. "Come quick! Please!"

"I'm coming. Is something—" Mrs. McGavock stopped in the doorway, eyes going wide, same as Miss Clouston's. "Oh my . . ."

"I think . . . the baby's coming," Aletta ground out, her legs giving way.

Jake caught her and lifted her in his arms.

"The Colonel's and my room upstairs," Mrs.

258

McGavock called. "And I'll ask the Colonel to ride for the doctor straightaway."

Aletta groaned as Jake carried her up the stairs and laid her on the bed. She felt the telltale rush of warmth issuing from her womb and closed her eyes, concentrating on breathing, the memory of Andrew's birth returning in vivid detail.

"Aletta"—Jake leaned close—"it's going to be all right. We're here with you."

She breathed through the contraction, feeling the pain begin to subside even while knowing it would return.

"I love you, Aletta. I want you to be my wife. And no matter how long you need, I'll wait for you. Do you hear me?"

"Of course I hear you," she finally whispered, opening her eyes. "I'm right here, after all."

With a wry smile, he cupped her face in his hands and kissed her, slow and deep. Already breathless, she filled her lungs and looked into his eyes.

"Jake, we might have to . . . delay that trip to town for a day or two."

"That's all right. It'll still be there."

Another pain began to build, and Aletta curled onto her side, fisting the bedcovers.

"Captain Winston!" Mrs. McGavock's voice rang out with authority. "It's time for you to leave now, sir. A woman in labor is not a woman of a mind to—"

"Jake," Aletta ground out, breathing through the pain, waiting for it to ease.

"Yes, my love, I'm here. I'm right here."

She reached for his hand and he held hers tight.

"You won't," she whispered, "have to wait for me long."

He pressed a kiss to her forehead just before Colonel Carrie and Tempy chased him from the room.

EPILOGUE

SIX MONTHS LATER
SUMMER 1864

"Very nicely done, Mrs. Winston."

Aletta smiled up at Jake, still loving when he called her that, and loving him more with each passing day. She eyed the piece of carved wood with leather straps in her hand, knowing it wasn't perfect. But also knowing it was a far cry better than her first attempt months ago.

Jake glanced back. "Emmett, are you ready to try out your new leg?"

"Am I ever, Captain. But I don't see how it could be any better than the one you both made me back in January."

Aletta came alongside them, reading the fresh hope in Kate's eyes. "That was one of our first attempts, Corporal Zachary. Which, when translated, means my husband and I were still learning." She laughed along with them. "We've managed to perfect a few more details since then."

She let Jake do the actual fitting, as he usually did, and true to what they'd thought, the new alteration they'd made to the leather strap on the artificial leg gave Emmett much greater mobility and ease of movement.

Jake's long-range sight had never improved, which made returning to battle an impossibility. That had bothered him, she knew. Because he loved his country, his fellow soldiers, and he wanted to contribute to the cause. But he was doing that. They both were. Together. Because they'd found new purpose. And with the pair of spectacles the doctor had recently supplied—quite handsome on her husband, she thought—Jake could see close up better than ever.

As Jake and Emmett spoke together and Kate looked on, Aletta pondered all that had happened in the last few months and just how grateful she was that God had chosen to bring such indescribable joy through such painful events in her life. Not that she didn't still have days when she missed Warren. She did. She would always carry his love inside her and would make certain that Andrew and little Gracie knew how much Warren—whose body she'd finally laid to rest in the town cemetery—had loved them.

Just as their father now loved them.

"I never would have dreamed, Aletta, that an

abandoned factory could feel so much like a home."

Aletta turned to Kate beside her. "Neither did I, at first. But when Jake shared his dream with me, when he told me the idea that God had put into his heart, I knew this was where we were supposed to be. And it's perfect for us. We still need to renovate the upper floor, which we hope to very soon. We want to use that to welcome and house wounded soldiers as they're finding their way again."

"Aletta?"

Hearing her name, Aletta turned to see MaryNell coming in through the business entrance, the swell in her friend's belly just beginning to show. Robert Goodall had returned on furlough in late January and Aletta smiled to herself—come October, little Seth would have a new baby brother or sister. MaryNell had chosen wisely. And as it turned out, she'd managed to keep their house too. Without the least assistance from Herbert Cornwall.

Once Emmett and Kate had left, and MaryNell had delivered yet another stack of orders for artificial limbs before heading home, Aletta and Jake took a moment to eat lunch together with the children at a front table.

Aletta's gaze drifted upward, as it so often did, to the newspaper clipping now framed over her workbench. The article Jake had written that appeared in the *Nashville Banner* shortly after Christmas. She read the first couple of paragraphs, already knowing them by heart, and a swell of pride for her husband moved through her.

"These women of the Women's Relief Society—these genteel, courageous females who fight a battle men have yet to endure—aren't merely knitting socks and sewing quilts as I'd first imagined. They're knitting this community together in a way it hasn't been before, and they're emboldening the hearts of their husbands and sons and fathers and brothers to surge ever forward in the battle for freedom and in the defense of love and honor for country. They're bearing each other's burdens and losses, sharing what they have with others who have none, and bringing fresh hope to thousands of soldiers in the Confederate Army. And, in the process, they're strengthening the very lifeblood of this town. Of this wounded nation. Something that never could have been accomplished if people had simply given money and then gone on their way, as I first, very mistakenly, recommended. I've never been more grateful to have been shown the error of my ways, and to have been a part—albeit, a small one—of an effort so noble, so rich with self-sacrifice that it hearkens with encouragement not only for the present . . . but for all eternity."

Author's Note

Dear friend,

Time is precious, and I appreciate you sharing yours with me—and with Jake and Aletta, the McGavock family of Carnton, Tempy, their cook, and the rest of the people from Franklin.

Jake and Aletta's characters are compilations of historical accounts I've read about sharpshooters from the Civil War and also of the many women who were widowed during the war. Their diaries and letters tell stories of immeasurable heartache and courage, and of faith in Christ who saw them through it all. So many of these women never received the opportunity to bury their husbands, sons, fathers, and brothers who fell on the battlefield. Because so many of the bodies lacked proper identification and were hastily buried. Tragically so.

Tempy's character is based on the real Carnton cook—an older African American woman—who was, indeed, left behind when all the other Carnton slaves were moved to various locations during the Civil War. Her real identity and name have been lost to time, but she came vividly to my imagination when I learned what little I could about her. And she's a character I look forward to including in the three upcoming Carnton novels, as are John and Carrie McGavock and their children, Hattie and Winder.

Women's Relief Societies were prevalent during the Civil War, both in the North and the South, and the activities I included in *Christmas at Carnton* are based on historical accounts of these societies and the enormous good they undertook to accomplish. One of those tasks being to provide artificial limbs for the wounded soldiers. When you're next in Nashville, I invite you to visit Carnton Plantation in Franklin, Tennessee. Not only to tour the home, but to walk the grounds and learn more about this slice of American history.

If you're part of a book club reading one of my books, I'd love to join your meeting via Skype for a twenty- to thirty-minute call. Visit the Bonus Features page on my website and click "For Book Clubs" for more details. Also, if you love making recipes from novels, visit the "Novel Recipes" link on that same page for more recipes.

Finally, you met two secondary characters in this story who are also from the pages of history—Captain Roland Ward Jones and Miss Elizabeth Clouston, the McGavock's nanny. Captain Roland Jones was wounded in the Battle of Franklin in December 1864 and was brought to Carnton, along with scores of other soldiers, which served as a hospital for the wounded. He and Elizabeth (Lizzie) met that night, and I look forward to sharing their real love story with you in the first installment of the Carnton novels.

Each month I offer exclusive giveaways to my newsletter friends. So be sure to sign up for that when you're visiting my website. I love hearing from you . . . so please, let's stay connected.

Much love until then,
Tamera

ACKNOWLEDGEMENTS

With gratitude to . . .

My family for supporting me in ways beyond measure.

Joanna Stephens (Carnton Curator) and Elizabeth Trescott (Carnton Collections Manager) for reading the first draft of this novella and for lending their historical expertise on Carnton and the McGavock family.

My editors Daisy Hutton, Becky Philpott, and Ami McConnell for asking all the right thought-provoking questions and for helping to bring the heart of this story into greater clarity.

Kristen Ingebretson for the gorgeous cover!

Natasha Kern, my literary agent, for your continual support and awesome friendship.

To my readers for embracing yet another historical setting and cast of characters, many of them taken from the pages of history. I treasure our connection and hope to see you at Carnton in Franklin, Tennessee, someday soon!

To my Lord and Savior Jesus Christ, through whom, because of his sacrifice, those who belong to him never truly have to say goodbye to each other. Only, goodbye for now—until we're all finally gathered Home. Thank you, Lord, for meeting me on the page, yet again. All glory is yours.

DISCUSSION QUESTIONS

1. What happened to Aletta—being widowed so young, already a mother and with another child on the way—was the norm rather than the exception during the Civil War. Over 620,000 soldiers were killed during the course of the war. Could you empathize with Aletta and her challenges? Her choices? Have you experienced the loss of a spouse? Could you relate to her grief and her difficulty in accepting the truth about her husband's death?

2. MaryNell, Aletta's friend, also faced a difficult choice. What did you feel toward MaryNell in her circumstances? And toward Aletta as she realized what decision her friend was facing?

3. Before reading *Christmas at Carnton*, were you aware of Women's Relief Societies and how women from both the South and the North created these organizations to support both the Confederate and Federal soldiers? Had you been living back then, do you think

you would have taken part in one of these societies? And in their auctions? Discuss the important role these organizations made in the lives of the soldiers and the differences they made to the women themselves.

4. Did you understand Jake's reluctance to be a part of the Women's Relief Society? How did you feel about the newspaper article espousing that women were "best suited for hearth and home" (a common—and even celebrated—Victorian view of the day)? Did you share Aletta's reaction to that statement? What were your impressions of Jake upon his arrival at Carnton?

5. Come Christmas and other holidays, we tend to especially miss those loved ones who've gone on before us. Can you relate to Aletta's "dreading" Christmas? Have you ever felt that way? If yes, share that experience. Read II Corinthians 5:1–10 and discuss what it means to be "swallowed up by life" as the Scripture is translated in the NLT Bible, as well as what the believer in Christ has to look forward to following the death of the earthly body.

6. As Aletta grows closer to Jake, she harbors fear. Describe her fear and what it stems

from. Could you relate? What finally overcomes her fear?

7. What did you think of Tempy's character and what she said to Aletta in reference to being "left behind" when the rest of the slaves were taken farther South? Were you aware that oftentimes the Federal Army wasn't all that concerned with freeing the slaves? In ch. 20, Tempy offers counsel to Aletta about her own marriage and about trusting God. Do you share Tempy's belief? Do you consider God trustworthy? Read Isaiah 26:4, Jeremiah 17:5–8, and 1 Timothy 4:9–10 and discuss.

8. What is the most important lesson Jake learned in the story? What about Aletta? How do you relate?

9. Who were your favorite characters in the novel? Favorite scenes? Any similarities among your group?

10. Besides the precious gift of God's beloved Son, what's the best Christmas gift you've ever received?

Be sure to take a group picture of your book club (holding up your books!) and share it with Tamera at TameraAlexander@gmail.com.

RECIPES FROM
Christmas at Carnton

Aletta's Southern Pecan Pie
(just like Jake's mama's)

1 stick butter, melted
1 cup light corn syrup
1 cup sugar
3 large eggs, slightly beaten
½ teaspoon lemon juice
1 teaspoon vanilla
Dash salt
1 cup chopped pecans (plus a few whole pecans
     for the top)
1 unbaked piecrust (recipe below)

Brown butter in saucepan over low heat until golden brown, being careful not to burn. Let cool. Place remaining ingredients in mixing bowl in order listed and combine well. Blend in browned butter and pour into unbaked piecrust. Bake at 425 degrees for 10 minutes, then reduce heat to 325 degrees and continue baking for 35 to 40 minutes.

Aletta's Old-Fashioned Pie Crusts
(makes two large crusts)

I've been using this wonderful piecrust for years. It freezes well (instructions on freezing below), so even if I need only one piecrust at the moment, I always use this recipe and freeze the second one for later.

1½ cups shortening
3 cups flour
1 egg
5 tablespoons ice water
1 tablespoon white vinegar
1 teaspoon salt

In large bowl, using a pastry cutter (or two knives will do the job), gradually work shortening into flour for 3 to 4 minutes until mixture resembles coarse meal. In small bowl, whip egg; add to flour/shortening mixture. Add ice water, vinegar, and salt. Stir gently until blended well.

Divide dough into two balls and place each into large sealable plastic bag. Using a rolling pin, slightly flatten each to about ½-inch thickness to make rolling easier later. Seal bags and place in freezer until needed. (If you're using the crusts immediately, it's still a good idea to let them chill in the freezer for 15 to 20 minutes. They'll be much easier to work with.)

To prepare crust, remove dough from freezer and allow to thaw for 15 minutes (if frozen). On well-floured surface, roll out dough, starting at center and working outward. Sprinkle flour over dough if it seems too moist. If dough starts to stick to countertop, use a metal spatula to gently scrape it up, then flip it over and continue rolling until ½ inch larger in diameter than your pie plate.

Using a spatula, carefully transfer dough to pie pan. (I sometimes fold my well-floured dough in half and then "unfold" it into the pie plate. Or you can lop it over your rolling pin.) Gently press dough against sides of pan, then crimp edge.

Andrew's Favorite Pumpkin Bread

3 cups sugar
1 cup water
1 cup vegetable oil
4 large eggs
1 (15-ounce) can pumpkin puree
3 cups flour
2 teaspoons baking soda
½ teaspoon baking powder
1½ teaspoons salt
1 teaspoon cinnamon
1 teaspoon cloves
1 teaspoon nutmeg
1 cup chopped pecans (or walnuts)

Mix all ingredients in large mixing bowl. Pour into three greased standard-size loaf pans and bake at 350 degrees for 1 hour. This no-fail recipe is wonderful on a cold winter's eve, especially when shared with someone you love.

Scrumptious Southern Shortbread

¾ cup butter at room temp (1½ sticks)
½ cup powdered sugar
¼ teaspoon vanilla
1½ cups flour (sifted)

Preheat oven to 325 degrees. Spray small (8- or 9-inch) cast iron skillet very lightly with nonstick cooking spray. Cream butter until light and fluffy. Add powdered sugar, then vanilla. Next, work in the flour. You can use an electric mixer, or you can get into the 1860s way of doing things and knead the dough on an unfloured surface until smooth.

Press dough into skillet and bake for 30 to 35 minutes until golden brown. Cool for 10 to 15 minutes, then flip pan over onto wooden cutting board. Cut shortbread into pieces while still warm; it will set up as it cools. Or serve warm. Yields 10 to 12 servings. And it really does. This recipe is rich and delicious!

Tempy's Old-Fashioned Butter Cookies

1 cup butter, softened
¾ cup sugar
2 large egg yolks (no whites)
1 teaspoon vanilla
2 cups flour
¼ teaspoon salt
Pecan halves

Combine butter, sugar, egg yolks, and vanilla in mixing bowl. Beat at medium speed, scraping bowl often, until well combined. Add flour and salt; beat at low speed, scraping bowl often, until well mixed. Shape dough into 1-inch balls and place 2 inches apart onto ungreased cookie sheets. Flatten balls to ¼ inch with bottom of glass dipped in sugar. Place pecan half in center of each cookie. Bake at 350 degrees for 10 to 12 minutes or until edges are lightly browned. Cool for 1 minute on cookie sheets; remove to cooling rack.

Variations:
• Use a decorative cookie stamp instead of the bottom of a glass.
• To make old-fashioned crescent cookies, use

almond extract instead of vanilla and crushed almonds instead of pecans. Delicious!

- This recipe also makes scrumptious thumbprint cookies. Add your favorite buttercream frosting on top and voilà! Another wonderful holiday cookie along with great memories when you involve the kids.

Aletta's Chocolate Cream Pie

2⅓ cups milk, separated
1 cup sugar
4 tablespoons flour
Dash salt
3 tablespoons cocoa
3 egg yolks, well beaten
1 teaspoon vanilla
1 tablespoon butter
1 baked 9-inch pie shell

Heat 2 cups milk to almost boiling, being careful not to burn. Mix sugar, flour, salt, and cocoa; stir dry mixture into ⅓ cup cold milk until well moistened. Add beaten egg yolks. Then add entire mixture to hot milk and cook until thickened, stirring constantly. Add vanilla and butter. Cool slightly before pouring into baked pie shell. Cover with basic meringue (recipe follows) and brown in oven.

Basic Meringue

3 egg whites
Dash salt
¼ teaspoon cream of tartar
6 tablespoons sugar

Beat egg whites, salt, and cream of tartar until stiff but not dry. Gradually add sugar; beat after each tablespoon until sugar is partially dissolved. Scoop onto pie, making sure to seal the edges. Bake at 325 degrees for 5 to 10 minutes, watching closely so as not to overbrown. Enjoy!

Carrie McGavock's Chow-Chow

Carrie McGavock's recipe for this cherished vegetable relish appeared in the *Tennessee Model Household Guide*. She noted, "Will keep for years."

2 pecks green cucumbers
½ peck green tomatoes
1 pint green peppers
½ peck onions
1 ounce celery seed
1 ounce white mustard seed
1 ounce turmeric
1 ounce whole cloves
3 tablespoons ground mustard
Grated horseradish and black pepper to taste
2 pounds brown sugar

Slice or chop vegetables fine, salt well, and hang in thin cloth to drip in eve. Next morning scald in weak vinegar, then squeeze, dry, and add strong vinegar.

Now what on earth is a peck, you might ask? I asked the same thing. A peck is one-fourth of a bushel. Does that help? No, it didn't help me much either. In dry measure, a peck is 8 quarts.

So when Peter Piper picked a peck of pickled peppers, exactly how many peppers did Peter Piper pick? That depends on the type of pepper, of course, but the answer would be somewhere between 10 and 14 pounds. So this recipe is *definitely* intended to be canned—unless you're making chow-chow for a very large crowd! Or, say, a hog killing or Women's Relief Christmas auction!

Thanks to the staff at Carnton for giving permission to share this family recipe.

Christmas Simmering Spices

3 (4-inch) cinnamon sticks
3 bay leaves
¼ cup whole cloves
1 lemon, halved
1 orange, halved
1 quart water

Combine all ingredients in teakettle or 2-quart saucepan. Bring to a boil, then reduce heat and simmer as long as desired. Check often and add more water as needed. Mixture may be cooled and stored in refrigerator for several days and then reheated. Simmering spices have long been used to help lend homes that warm and cozy feeling come the holidays. Just like Tempy's kitchen!

ABOUT THE AUTHOR

Tamera Alexander is a *USA Today* bestselling novelist whose deeply drawn characters, thought-provoking plots, and poignant prose resonate with readers worldwide. She and her husband make their home in Nashville, not far from Carnton.

Tamera invites you to visit her at:

Website: TameraAlexander.com
Twitter: @TameraAlexander
Faccbook: Tamcra.Alcxandcr
Pinterest: TameraAuthor
Group Blog: InspiredbyLifeandFiction.com

Or if you prefer snail mail, please write her at:
Tamera Alexander
P.O. Box 871
Brentwood, TN 37024

Discussion questions for all of Tamera's novels are available at TameraAlexander.com, as are details about Tamera joining your book club for a virtual visit.

Books are produced in the United States using U.S.-based materials

Books are printed using a revolutionary new process called THINKtech™ that lowers energy usage by 70% and increases overall quality

Books are durable and flexible because of smythe-sewing

Paper is sourced using environmentally responsible foresting methods and the paper is acid-free

Center Point Large Print
600 Brooks Road / PO Box 1
Thorndike, ME 04986-0001 USA

(207) 568-3717

US & Canada:
1 800 929-9108
www.centerpointlargeprint.com